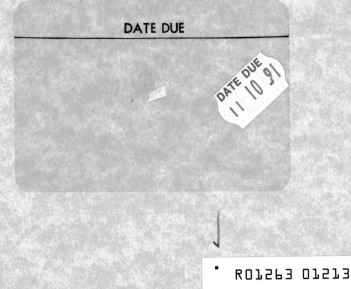

PARCHMENT HOUSE

PARCHMENT HOUSE

CARA LOCKHART SMITH

FOUR WINDS PRESS
New York

Four Winds Press
Macmillan Publishing Company
866 Third Avenue, New York, NY 10022
Collier Macmillan Canada, Inc.
First published in Great Britain 1989 by Methuen Children's Books, London
First American Edition 1989   Printed in the United States of America

10   9   8   7   6   5   4   3   2   1

Library of Congress Cataloging-in-Publication Data
Smith, Cara Lockhart.
Parchment House / Cara Lockhart Smith.
p.   cm.
Summary: In a desolate orphanage in futuristic Britain,
orphan Johnnie Rattle pits his wits against those of the
orphanage director, the cruel Reverend Slipper.
ISBN 0-02-785845-6
[1. Orphans—Fiction. 2. Robots—Fiction.] I. Title.
PZ7.S643.37Par 1989   [Fic]—dc19
89-1369   CIP   AC

FOR MATTY BYFIELD · AND FOR JAMIE AND SAM

CONTENTS

1

PARCHMENT HOUSE

There was nothing spectacular about the outside of Parchment House, nothing that would have let a passerby guess what went on inside. True, there were bars on the attic windows, but they might have been put there to keep small children from leaning out too far and breaking their necks on the ground beneath.

On a wooden signboard by the gate, and on a brass plate beside the front door, were written the words:

PARCHMENT HOUSE
HOME FOR
ORPHANED AND ABANDONED
CHILDREN

There were few passersby to read these words, as the house was set beside a lonely road on the outskirts of the seaside town of Carstairs and Bungho. But if anyone had been passing by, on one particular summer evening, and had happened to glance up toward the attic windows, they might have seen the face of a wild-looking boy.

This boy was Johnnie Rattle.

Johnnie Rattle was not supposed to be in the attic. He was supposed to be downstairs attending to the gadgets that cluttered up the whole of the ground floor. But he had grown tired of overhauling the Main Control Panel in the kitchen. The sun was shining, and yet he knew he could not go out into the open air, no matter how hard he worked, for it was forbidden.

In a sudden rage, he threw his oily rag in the sink and ran upstairs.

It was quiet in the attic, with only the sound of a seagull screaming around the roof. Johnnie leaned against the window frame and stared out through the dirty glass. Far off, across the heath, he could make out the factory chimneys of Carstairs and Bungho smoking against the sea. He wished he could fly out of the window. It would be better to be a sparrow, picking up crumbs on a cobbled pavement beside the docks, than be a child in Parchment House.

He fell into a daze, so he did not hear footsteps coming up the stairs.

A man stepped into the attic. It was Reverend Slipper, one of the Worthies in charge of Parchment House.

"Aha!" said the Reverend, getting Johnnie by the scruff of the neck and hauling the boy around to face him.

"Johnnie Rattle! I might have known! What do you think you are doing up here?"

An odd smell came off Reverend Slipper. Not a human smell—more like spilled chemicals. Johnnie stared up into the bony yellow face. The man let go of him and drew back.

"Who do you think you are, staring at me like that with those wicked black eyes of yours? Why, with your grubby-looking skin, and that hair that would be better suited to a scrubbing brush than a child, you look like a gypsy. Or worse. How dare you!"

Johnnie did not say a word.

"It is a great pity," said the Reverend, "that the Constitution of Parchment House does not allow one to beat some sense into orphans. But when you get sent off to be a Missionary Orphan, other rules will apply. I have a vision! I can see it all—a desert, a stretch of golden sand, some camels, a few palms, and lo and behold, right in the middle of it all, a nice, clean, shiny gallows, just set up for a certain kind of person! A person just like you, Johnnie Rattle! Woe betide you, when you are sent off to be a Missionary Orphan, if you have not mended your ways!"

"I am not going to be a Missionary Orphan."

"*What* did you say?"

"I am never ever under any circumstances going to be a Missionary Orphan."

"What delusion are you suffering from?" cried Reverend Slipper. "Every child who leaves Parchment House becomes a Missionary Orphan. *Every single one!*"

"Not me!" said Johnnie Rattle.

"Now look here," said Reverend Slipper, "we do not recognize this kind of thing."

A piece of ragged curtain hung beside the window.

The Reverend plucked at it and held it under Johnnie's nose. The netting smelled of dead flies.

"You see this piece of rag? Look how it hangs here, soiled with the vile fingers of a host of filthy orphans. See how thin it is. Look how easily it tears. . . ." Reverend Slipper put his bony finger into a hole in the curtain. "See how easily it turns to dust. Well, an orphan is of as much account as this piece of rag. Just as dirty. Just as useless. Just as easily destroyed. If I needed to tear an orphan I could tear one just . . . like . . . *that!*" said the Reverend, ripping downward through the net.

From far below on the ground floor came the sound of a whistle. The other orphans were being summoned for their evening mugs of nettle broth.

"You can do without supper," said Reverend Slipper. "You can stay up here and concentrate on the idea that it is only through the generosity of worthy people that you survive at all. Now, get to your cubicle!"

As Johnnie pulled the curtains of his cubicle he could hear Reverend Slipper's steps banging down the attic stairs.

The attic was where the orphans lived when they were not having lessons or cleaning gadgets. The long space was divided up into thirteen cubicles. Johnnie's was right up at the end, against the side wall of the house. Inside this cubicle were two secret things . . . a window and a geranium.

The window was set high up in the side wall of the house. It was round, and so small that it could hardly be seen from the inside, and not at all from the outside, hidden as it was by the shadow of the roof. The glass was old, and in places gave a rippled view of the landscape, as if it was seen through water. Each warp in the glass gave the view beyond a different slant. Out there,

4

fields stretched away toward a small forest on the horizon. The top of a tower could be seen above the trees, far off but distinct, the weathercock on its pointed roof silhouetted against the sky. Did anyone live there, all alone in the middle of the forest? Sometimes Johnnie thought he saw a light flashing from the top of the tower, as if someone, a child maybe, was sending out messages with a mirror or a flashlight.

The geranium was the other secret thing. Johnnie had found it a year ago hidden in the corner of the schoolroom window. The stalk had grown thick and nubby, but from it sprouted fresh, crinkled leaves and flowers on long stems. He loved the musty smell of the plant and the way its bright red flowers lit up the shabby cubicle. He felt the geranium was the only thing in the world that really belonged to him.

After Reverend Slipper had left, Johnnie knelt on his bed and gazed out of the secret window for a few minutes, to see if the light was flashing, but the tower was only a dark smudge against the late afternoon sky.

He sat down on the bed and picked up the geranium. New buds were appearing from a whorl of young leaves. He fed the plant a little dusty water from a cup by his bed and put it back on the floor. Then he stretched out on the bed and stared at the ceiling, trying to pretend he was far away. He could remember nothing, nothing at all, of any life before Parchment House, though it did seem that once, long ago, there had been a place where there had been food, and trees, and a house with unlocked doors. But had such a place really existed, or was it all in his imagination? In any case, it made no difference now. He lay motionless, thinking of nothing at all. He heard the cry of the rag-and-bone man passing along the road below, and the sound of the horse's hooves, and the trundling of the cart. The sounds gradually faded. Above the roof the gull screamed once more, then seemed to flap off somewhere else.

At last he fell asleep and dreamed he was a bird, flying far away, toward the sea.

After working all day on the Gadget Overhaul, the rest of the orphans were being given their weekly washing session in the bathroom. The rusty bath was filled with tepid water, and each child was scrubbed by Mrs. Padlock with a long-handled brush that had been soaked in a pail of disinfectant. Mrs. Padlock, a solid woman with a ginger wig and little eyes like beads, was the second-in-command to Reverend Slipper. She had a strong dislike of children, especially dirty ones.

Tacked on to the bathroom walls were homilies written in orange script on laminated green and lilac scrolls, for Mrs. Padlock and Reverend Slipper felt that no hour of the day was unsuitable for Moral Instruction. The homilies declared such things as "A Pure Skin And A Pure Heart" "Cleanliness Is Next To Godliness" "Scrub Away Those Sinful Ways." There was even a poem:

> *Humbleness and obedience,*
> *A merry merry heart,*
> *All these must I imbibe,*
> *And then to others happily impart.*

The children did not read these texts, but sat hunched up, their heads bent toward the gray water while they were scrubbed. All, that is, except Tiggy, who tried to bite Mrs. Padlock on the arm, and Grub, who would not stay in the bath at all, but jumped out of the water and ran around the room shouting: "Oh, oh, oh, I wanna banana . . . gimme a sausage . . . gimme a banana . . . I feel empty inside!"

"A banana! A sausage! You little heathen!"

Mrs. Padlock forced Grub, still all wet, into some clean clothes from the communal pile kept in the linen cupboard. "Now mind you take off the top layer before you get into bed. Be off with you!"

She counted on her fingers to see who had been done: Tiggy and Grub, the thin Twins, Philadelphia Lemon, Anna and Jackie Daw, whimpering Alice, Johnnie Rattle confined to the attic, leave him out, Jane Pegg, Percival with his own little bath, leave him out, eleven down, two to go—Solly Turk and Inky Dumb-Dumb.

She opened the door. There stood Solly Turk, but no Inky Dumb-Dumb. Solly was scowling at her. The insolence! But then what could you expect from a child who had only just arrived at Parchment House, due to his father having taken to being a tramp? Parchment House would soon teach the brat to wipe that brazen look off his face!

Mrs. Padlock decided, however, not to give Solly a bath, but just handed him a pile of clothes. The boy looked down at them in disgust.

"What do you expect?" said Mrs. Padlock. "Clothes of your own? You'll be wanting a wardrobe next! Where is the other child?"

"Inky Dumb-Dumb is ill."

"Ill? What do you mean, ill? Go and bring him here immediately!"

"I don't know where he is."

But Mrs. Padlock had made out a kind of shuffling noise outside in the corridor. She flung open the door and caught Inky Dumb-Dumb trying to crawl up the stairs to the attic.

Mrs. Padlock seized on Inky and bundled him into

7

the bathroom, hitting Solly away with the brush. She locked the door.

"I suppose you think you're too good for tenth-hand water, do you? *Do you?* Why do you never speak? I'll show you!"

Inky Dumb-Dumb lay in a huddle, not moving. Only his eyes looked up out of the heap of dark clothes. She stripped him and hauled him into the bath, and she kept him in there even longer than the others. Then she sent him crawling up to the attic.

The ground floor of Parchment House (where the four Worthies—Reverend Slipper, Mrs. Padlock, Miss Stir, and big Marvin—spent most of the day) smelled of polish and chrome and plastic flowers. But up in the attic, there was a moldy smell, which was never completely blown away by the threads of wind that crept under the windowsills and through the cracks between the floorboards.

The children's cubicles were separated from each other by rummage sale curtains. Inside each cubicle (except for one) was an old bed and an old mattress, covered with two horse blankets and a lumpy pillow. There was little else. The children had nothing but a few meager treasures they had managed to pick up here and there: striped and speckled stones; a shard of blue china; some bones; a scrap of wool. The only cubicle that was nice was up at the end, next to Johnnie Rattle. This cubicle had purple velvet curtains, a red carpet, a neat little white bed, and a padlocked fridge. The rest of the attic was threadbare and cold.

Gradually the place filled up with scrubbed and weary children. Apart from some crying from the younger ones, there was scarcely any noise. Even up

8

here, away from the Worthies, the orphans were never boisterous.

Anna Daw picked up her brother.

"Oh, Jackie, do stop hollering, you'll get us all beaten. Now take your magic stone and get in under the blankets."

She tucked him in, but the boy had been polishing the Executive Tea Maker all day, and now, as he fell asleep, he kept rubbing his cheek with one fist, while the other clutched his magic stone.

Anna shuffled around, getting the younger ones to bed. The thin Twins slipped under the blankets, still chattering away in the language they used to each other and no one else. But the sound was getting softer and softer, and only the tops of their bony heads still showed above the bedding. Tiggy bounced on her bed mouthing: "I'm a tiger, I'm a tiger!" until she fell off and banged her head on the iron bed leg, whereupon she immediately crawled into the bed and fell asleep. Grub was still mumbling about sausages in his dreams, and Alice was sniffing into her pillow.

Philadelphia Lemon, a lanky, worried-looking girl, leaned over a heap by the door.

"Come on, Inky, don't lie there all night. What's the matter?"

The boy was shaking all over.

"Are you ill, Inky? What is it? Come on, get into bed."

She tried to coax him, but he shrank away, and all the time he kept his head cocked sideways against his chest like an injured bird, staring up at her with one expressionless eye. Philadelphia gave up. She took one of the blankets off his bed, wrapped it around him, and left him alone.

9

When the younger children were in bed, the others gathered around the window that looked out over the front lawn, that lawn where they were never allowed to play. They did not want to go to bed until the sun had completely vanished. The grass outside shone almost red-gold beyond the great shadow of the house.

Solly Turk was rubbing the top of his bristly head in a fury, as if Mrs. Padlock and the Reverend Slipper were fleas he wanted to scrub out of his hair.

"Them downstairs with them gadgets of theirs," he groused. "They need an automatic whatsit to pick their noses for them. *I'd* like to get an automatic whatsit to knock their heads off, I would, I'm telling you. I hate gadgets, and I hate Worthies. I do, I do!"

The children thought about all the contraptions they had been overhauling: the Doughnut Extruder, the Soothibooths, the Feather Dusteroo, the Whizzibars— not to mention the Kleenukwik, the Vizibox, and the Birdsong and Proverb Broadcaster.

"But gadgets are funny when they go wrong," said Philadelphia Lemon. "Do you remember when the sandwiches came shooting out of the Kleenukwik all covered with bubbles?"

"Or that time when the Feather Dusteroo knocked the heads off all Mrs. Padlock's china cherubs?"

"Or when the Soothibooth tore all her hair off?"

"But what about that time you told me of, when the water turned green and them frogs came down the tap?" said Solly.

"Oh, that was wonderful!"

(If Johnnie Rattle had been awake this would have made him smile, for he knew all about frogs and green water. Gadgets went wrong anyway, but they went wronger with a bit of help. All you had to do was twist a knob a little too far, reroute a wire, fiddle with a thermostat, and hey, presto! All the delicate mechanisms went haywire. Yes, fouling up gadgets was an art!)

The children looked out of the window, watching the shadows spreading until there was nothing to be made out at all. The attic grew dark.

"It's very bad, though. It's very bad," said Philadelphia.

"We're treated worse than stray dogs. At least they can run around and scavenge," said Anna, scratching at the peeling window frame.

"We ought to write to somebody. The Mayor. The Governors. There must be somebody out there."

"Oh, ha-ha," said Solly, "oh, ha-ha-ha. Them outside want us in here *in* here. What do they care what happens to us? We're just useless orphans what is living at others' expense. *You* know how it is."

"You're not an orphan, you're an abandoned child," said Anna Daw.

"Left, not abandoned," said Solly.

"And we couldn't get a stamp," said Jane Pegg, who scarcely ever dared to say a word.

"No, Jane, you're right," said Anna. "We can't even get out to play on the lawn. How could we mail a letter?"

"Oh, it's useless, useless," Philadelphia suddenly cried, tugging at her long pigtail with her bony hand as if she was trying to pull her own head off. "Nothing works, nothing at all. We're just prisoners. In the end we'll be sent away to the Empire to become Missionary Orphans and never be heard of again. For all we know Missionary Orphans just get eaten by crocodiles. If there was a way out some orphan in the past would have thought of it. Why should we be different? It's forever and ever, all this!"

The other children were terrified by these words.

"Oh, don't, Philly, please don't," said Anna, pulling

11

at her hand. "Come on, let's sleep. We can get away from here when we're dreaming."

She led the tall girl away. Gradually the others drifted to their cubicles. The attic grew quiet.

Much later, when it was well past midnight, the door creaked open and a portly boy in pajamas stepped in, carrying a flashlight and a big handful of candy. He waddled down the attic to the nice cubicle next to Johnnie Rattle. This boy was Percival Amalgam. Percival was privileged. He did not have to work on gadgets or attend lessons, but lounged about all day, eating and watching the Vizibox in Mrs. Padlock's room. At night he lay in his cubicle and listened and munched, munched and listened. Then later he would relay snippets of information to the Worthies. The key to the padlocked fridge was on a thin gold chain hidden in the folds beneath his chin.

Percival Amalgam was a spy.

2

"THE EMPIRE IS A DUMP!"

After Gadget Overhaul Day, it was Empire Lecture Day.

The Constitution, where the Aims and Ideals of Parchment House were laid out, said that all Waifs and Strays should be turned into Missionary Orphans and sent far and wide into the territories of the Empire. On page two it was expressly stated: "Carstairs and Bungho is Ever Mindful of the Welfare of the Heathen."

To this end the children were instructed in Morality, Geography, Citizenship, and the History of Empire.

The schoolroom was dusty. The desks were

bleached and cracked with age. The walls were covered by old maps, with the Empire marked out in brown, some yellowish photographs of distant mission stations, and also two framed letters in spidery writing which said how useful ex-orphans had proved and how sorely they would be missed.

Mrs. Padlock, in a dress covered with khaki flowers, and a magenta sweater, sat at a small table on a raised platform in front of the class. When the orphans were sitting quietly behind their desks, she rapped on her table and began to speak of the exploits of the Gaberdine soldiers in suppressing an uprising in the Ganda Ganda Territories. She was telling for the umpteenth time about the wonderful Boon of Empire shown toward ungrateful natives when Solly Turk, who until now had been gazing out of the window, suddenly turned his head and shouted, *"This Empire stuff is rubbish!"*

"What?" screamed Mrs. Padlock.

"My dad says there ain't no Empire no more," went on Solly Turk, "and there never will be again, and there shouldn't of been one in the first place, so there!"

"Nobody," said Mrs. Padlock, swelling up in her chair like a Yorkshire pudding in a hot oven, *"nobody* could possibly want to know what your irresponsible father had to say before he disappeared from your life, leaving you here to live on charity. Where do you think Missionary Orphans go when they pass for the last time beneath these protective portals? The Empire is as bright as the sun, as deep as the sea, as everlasting as . . ."

"Oh, no it isn't," shouted back Solly. "It's you telling us them lies what you always tell."

Then all the orphans began to yell at Mrs. Padlock.

"The Empire is a monstrosity!"

"It's piffle!"

"It's pathetic!"

"The Empire is a dump, a dump, a dump!"

And then, remembering their own lost families, they began to shout about all the things *their* dads and moms had said once upon a time before Parchment House. "I wanna . . . wanna . . . wanna . . . I wanna *go home!*" wailed Grub and hurled himself on the floor, while Solly Turk climbed on to his desk and stamped his heels and whooped. And most surprising of all, timid Jane Pegg tore a piece of paper out of her Empire notebook, folded it into a dart, dipped it into the inkwell, and threw it in the direction of Mrs. Padlock.

The dart flew as if magnetized and landed in the middle of the magenta sweater. Mrs. Padlock sank backward. Her face went gray beneath her brick red powder. Then, banging her fist on the table so hard a cloud of dust rose into the air, she shrieked, *"I cannot . . . Really . . . Disgraceful . . . Oh, this is too much . . . Hideous, ungrateful hooligans!"*

Her face turned scarlet, and she tottered from the room.

For a few minutes there was pandemonium. The orphans stampeded around the schoolroom. Only Inky Dumb-Dumb did not move, but stayed hunched up at his desk, shivering and staring at the wood. Suddenly there was a coldness in the air. In the doorway, grim as a dead crow, stood Reverend Slipper. Everybody froze.

"Aha," said Reverend Slipper. "What a pity that corporal punishment is disallowed by the Constitution. All I can suggest is confinement and a severe fast for a week. Water and crumbs and nothing else at all. And Ablution Duty every day for Solly Turk for instigating this uproar."

"Ugh," said Solly.

Ablution Duty meant cleaning from top to bottom

the bathing machines of Mrs. Padlock and the Reverend Slipper. The machines were clogged with lather and grease and jellified soap and toenail fragments and hair. It was a nasty job—one kept as a special punishment.

Reverend Slipper had not finished. He stood before the orphans, staring at each face in turn.

"Mrs. Padlock has been grievously assaulted by some child here. Her sweater is fit only for the Garbage Disposal. Now, I wish to know—*who threw the dart?*"

There was silence. All the children stared at Reverend Slipper as if they were turned to stone.

"You see," said Reverend Slipper in a soft voice, "I must know. For future reference. I must know who harbors this terrible potential for violence within his or her breast. *I must know!*"

A sound like a suppressed hiccup came from Jane Pegg. Johnnie looked sideways at her. The girl was completely white and her eyes looked as if they were starting out of her head.

"I threw the dart," said Johnnie.

A sigh ran through the children. Reverend Slipper gave Johnnie a terrible stare, but said no more than, "You, too, shall do Ablution Duty. And I shall keep the incident on file."

The Reverend spent the rest of the day reading to the children from an exhaustive history of the early years of Parchment House, then sent them to their cubicles to begin the week-long fast.

It was early evening. The orphans were in the attic, starting their week's confinement and fast. Exhausted, the Reverend felt he had no energy left for Moral Meditation in his study. "I shall take a little stroll around the vegetable garden," he said to himself, "and ponder on Nature's Bounty. I'll go and inspect the Bird Table."

Birds were the Reverend's hobby. Often in the morning he would take the air gun and try a few pot shots at the starlings strutting about the place. Or he would go out and disentangle the dead titmice and pick up the poisoned finches. Occasionally he was even lucky enough to have an escaped parakeet or an errant canary wandering into the garden. All added to the Feather Bags. For Reverend Slipper collected feathers.

The whole of a little pantry off the kitchen was full of sacks of feathers. Blue, green, yellow, and even a few red were kept in leather pouches. Black and white and brown and speckled were stored in large sacks. The leftover bones were left separately in more sacks behind the pagoda at the end of the vegetable garden. If the Reverend nabbed a pigeon or a magpie it was turned directly into pies or soup and given to the orphans. It was gratifying to feel that they were thus provided with useful vitamins at no extra cost. Reverend Slipper did not, however, allow himself to try these delicacies. Shambles Methuselah, the gardener, cooked for the orphans. The Worthies' food was provided by the gadgets. The very smell of maggoty pie made the Reverend feel queasy.

The Parchment House Bird Table pretended to be harmless, indeed to be an encouragement to birds. It had been made from an old pool table. It used up a large area of the vegetable garden, down beside the hedge. It had gone to wrack and ruin, and now its stained green cloth toned nicely with the surroundings. Who was to know that the pockets were not only useful nut holders, but concealed rigged traps for little birds, and that the seed was poisoned?

On this summer evening, as the Reverend strolled around the vegetables, swallows zipped above his head. Swallows had nice feathers, but were not catchable.

There were no other birds about. There were no captives on the Bird Table. He was about to stroll back into the house when he saw a scrap of paper caught in the tangle of weeds under the table.

Sighing with annoyance, he picked it up, reminding himself to admonish Shambles about litter the next time he saw him. He was about to tear the paper into pieces and throw it over the hedge when the name of the Useful Machine Factory (Robots) Ltd. caught his eye.

The Useful Machine Factory (Robots) Ltd. was a company set up by the Opportunities Scheme, after the Great Recession, in a converted prison down by the docks. It was the principal source of gadgets for Parchment House. The piece of paper announced their latest invention, offering it at a reduced rate to anyone applying before the thirty-first of July.

In spite of his exhaustion, Reverend Slipper read the flier carefully.

The orphans were obviously getting dangerously uppity. Anarchy itself threatened the Constitution of Parchment House. If there was one thing the Reverend could not stand it was Anarchy. The very word made him feel nauseous. Why, with the slightest encouragement from that pip-squeak Grub, or that fiend Johnnie Rattle, the orphans might begin to think they had been put on earth to do exactly what they liked. Perish the thought! If the flier was true to its promises, then Anarchy could be dealt with once and for all.

Reverend Slipper heard the distant whistle from the factory down in the town, the whistle that said the working day was over. "And our working day is never done," he sighed. He put the flier in his big pocket and took one more stroll around the vegetables, whistling softly to himself to the tune of "Fight On, Fight On, Till Dark Be Gone," and feeling suddenly calm.

3
ARCHIBALD!

The next day, Reverend Slipper summoned all the Worthies to a meeting in the front room. Mrs. Padlock came bustling in, followed by Miss Stir, a strong-looking woman in overalls. Big Marvin was already there, sound asleep in the corner. His black, weather-beaten suit, which looked as if it had not been taken off for a week, hung in crumples around him, and his face was hidden by a mat of hair. Mrs. Padlock glared at big Marvin. The man resembled an old yak. She would like to sweep him up with the Feather Dusteroo! What with him, and

Miss Stir in her oil-stained overalls, the whole tone of Parchment House was brought down a peg. And what did he have to sleep about, she'd like to know? He never did a thing; he wasn't fit to be a Worthy. But her tuts and sighs made no impression whatsoever on the figure in the corner, which just slept on, snoring gently to itself in the corner armchair.

Reverend Slipper placed the flier on an end table. In slightly smudged black lettering it said:

THE USEFUL MACHINE FACTORY (ROBOTS) LTD.
PROUDLY PRESENTS
A PHIRST, PHINAL, PHANTASTIC OFFER!
THE ONE YOU DARE NOT MISS!
HERE HE IS

ARCHIBALD!!

THE ONE AND ONLY SELF-MOTIVATING ROBOT!
THIS IS WHAT YOU HAVE ALL BEEN WAITING
FOR—THE ROBOT THAT FEELS THE ROBOT THAT DEALS
YES THAT'S RIGHT DEALS WITH *YOUR* PROBLEMS!

ARCHIE CAN DO ARITHMETIC GEOMETRY TRIGONOMETRY
DIFFERENTIAL CALCULUS QUANTUM PHYSICS PICTURE
APPRECIATION CARPENTRY KNITTING AND NEEDLEWORK

ARCHIE CAN ACT AS GUARD DOG PEDAGOGUE GODFATHER
CAN BABY-SIT ANY INFANT FROM AGE THIRTY-SIX
MONTHS **ARCHIE** CAN DO ANYTHING YOU CAN DO
AND MORE MORE MORE LEAVING YOU ALL THAT
TIME TO DO ALL THE THINGS YOU'VE ALWAYS
WANTED TO DO BUT NEVER THOUGHT YOU COULD!

SO . . . SEND FOR ARCHIE!!!

WE KNOW OF NO RIVALS IN THE FIELD—
IF YOU FIND ANYTHING THAT MATCHES **ARCHIE**

WE MAKE YOU A GREAT OFFER—YOUR MONEY
BACK AND NO QUESTIONS ASKED—THIS IS
                    OUR PROMISE TO *YOU*!

THIS OFFER WILL NEVER BE REPEATED. PLEASE SEND
SELF-ADDRESSED ENVELOPE FOR FURTHER DETAILS AND
FREE TRIAL WITH NO OBLIGATION TO:
THE USEFUL MACHINE FACTORY (ROBOTS) LTD.,
THE DOCKS, CARSTAIRS AND BUNGHO CA13 7FU

"To me, it is the answer to a prayer. It is the perfect solution," said Reverend Slipper.

"To what?" said Miss Stir. "And what about the money?" she added, scratching her gray hair in irritation, then searching in the pocket of her overalls for a cigar. "And would it be . . . safe?"

"Safe? For whom?" said the Reverend. "Negative thoughts, Miss Stir, negative thoughts. And as for cost, we can put half down as equipment and half as staff salary. For that is what the robot will be, an extra pair of hands. *Firm* hands. And also a brain. A *brain,* Miss Stir."

"If I might put in my penny's worth of opinion," said Mrs. Padlock. "I would suggest we all threaten a strike if we can't have one of these. Orphans roaming unsupervised around the streets of Carstairs and Bungho at the height of the holiday season won't please the Authorities."

"If Archibald is a success," said the Reverend, "then we shall have more time to attend to our proper duties. We might even get away for a small holiday ourselves. That is to say, you and I, Mrs. Padlock. I'm sure you wouldn't mind, would you, Miss Stir? I'm sure a hotel with potted palms and humble porters is not at all your cup of tea. You would be much better off keeping the home fires burning here. You could take a few health-

21

giving walks while we are away. The air down by the docks is very bracing, I believe."

"A holiday! A dream come true!" cried Mrs. Padlock.

Miss Stir said nothing, but took a small booklet entitled *Your Wrench: How To Make It Work For You* out of her pocket and began to read the introduction.

"Right, that's settled," continued the Reverend. "I think we should move fast in this matter before we are thwarted by other interested parties. Let us take a vote."

Miss Stir abstained on principle. Reverend Slipper looked with distaste at the sleeping form in the corner. Try as he might, he could not work out how big Marvin had come to be a Worthy. The man looked as if he had fallen out of a broom cupboard.

"Miss Stir, could you prod him and see if he can be persuaded to vote."

But before Miss Stir could move, big Marvin suddenly got up and lumbered out of the room, not looking to right or left.

"I would almost take him for a tramp," said Mrs. Padlock in a high voice, looking nervously at the unclosed door.

"Oh, never mind. The vote is carried unanimously," said Reverend Slipper. He had already written a letter to the Useful Machine Factory (Robots) Ltd. Stamped and addressed, it lay on his blotter. He went to his study and rang for the gardener.

"Take this to the main post office before it closes, Shambles. Now run along, and on your way out, push the button for my tea. Two sugars with cream, mind you, and a selection of jam doughnuts."

Shambles went off to Carstairs and Bungho on his motor scooter, forgetting all about pushing the button, so the Reverend had to deal with it himself. Moreover, the gardener, after mailing the letter, went and drank cider all evening in The Pig and Firework and ended up sleeping in a ditch, so there was no one to press the button for the Worthies' breakfast either.

The sooner Archibald puts in an appearance, the better it will be for everybody, thought the Reverend.

After the week's punishment fast, the orphans were very weak. Inky Dumb-Dumb sat in a corner, chewing the edge of his sleeve. The others lay on their beds, dreaming odd dreams, sometimes even imagining themselves back in their old homes, with their families still around them. As for Percival Amalgam, he kept out of the way, in case they might be tempted to steal his tidbits. He spent all day in Mrs. Padlock's room, watching game shows on the Vizibox.

It was the last day of the fast. Up in the attic the air smelled sour. Only Solly Turk was not dozing, but was standing by the window, banging out a rhythm on the empty radiator with a couple of nails he had pulled out of the floorboards:

tap tap tap-tap-tap *tap tap*
tap-tap-tap *tap tap tap*

Johnnie lay in his cubicle with the curtains closed. The smell of the Ablution Machines still seemed to cling to his clothes. He had a strange feeling in his head, as if it had gone muzzy at the edges. He felt as if time had stopped, as if it would always be this grayish summer's day, as if Solly Turk would tap-tap-tap on the empty radiator forever. Suddenly, the noise stopped. The sound of muttering stopped too. Then Solly barged into Johnnie's cubicle.

"Come and look out the front. Something's happening!"

The orphans all crowded to the windows and looked down.

At the gate was a van quite unlike the usual sleek delivery trucks. There was no name written on it. Its mudguards were dirty and there was a layer of dust reaching halfway up the sides. The driver and Miss Stir were unloading several squarish white packages. Then they dragged out a bulky object all swathed in dust sheets and carried it up the path, watched by Mrs. Padlock and Reverend Slipper. Even big Marvin was there, standing a little aside, with his foot in a flower bed, appearing to be examining his nails.

When all the packages had been unloaded and carried to the house the Worthies went back inside, closing the front door with a bang. The van turned around and went back in the direction of Carstairs and Bungho.

For several minutes the children all stayed crowded up at the windows, staring down into the garden as if hypnotized. But nothing more happened. A few strips of packaging blew across the scuffed gravel. The orphans' breath started to mist up the glass. Grub was chewing at the old net curtain. The thin Twins gabbled in excited whispers, but the other children looked more thoughtful.

"It's a . . . it's a . . . what is it?" said Tiggy.

"It looked like a body, all wrapped up," said Solly, and Jackie Daw started crying.

Some sparrows started to peck at the packaging and then flew off. Philadelphia Lemon opened the attic door and listened, but there was complete silence down below.

One by one the children drifted back to their cubicles and once more stretched out on their beds. They didn't know why, but they felt uneasy. Something was different about this new delivery to Parchment House.

Solly Turk and Johnnie Rattle stayed for a while by the window, mulling over what they had seen.

"I just have a feeling," said Johnnie, "that something is going to happen."

"Sinister, weren't it, that thing down there."

"Very."

"Well," said Solly, "we's soon going to find out all about it, *that's* for sure."

A full moon shone that night. Parchment House threw a big square shadow. The magnolia trees threw tangled shadows on the front lawn. Moths jigged up and down the vegetable garden. In the pagoda at the end of the vegetable garden, Shambles Methuselah slept wrapped in several copies of *The Social Whirl* and an army coat, his head on a sack of lawn clippings.

In the attic all the orphans were asleep. Except one. Johnnie Rattle sat up suddenly, his mouth dry. The orphans had broken their fast that evening by being given ham-fat soup for supper, and it had been very salty. Johnnie realized he was parched with thirst. He lay down again and tried to sleep, but when he dozed off he dreamed of rain falling on a river, and woke up even more thirsty than before. His mouth felt as if it was made of sandpaper.

Every so often, when no one was paying attention, Johnnie sneaked into the laundry or the kitchen and filled a cup with water for his geranium. The empty cup, with a dead fly in it, was lying on its side by the bed. He wondered if he dared creep down and fill it up. He would have to go all the way down to the kitchen, as the taps on the middle floor made a terrible groaning noise when they were turned on. The kitchen seemed a long way off. But it was no good. . . . He could stand the thirst no longer.

Soon he was up and out of bed and down the first flight of stairs. Now came the tricky part—the Worthies' bedrooms. He tiptoed past the doors toward the second flight of stairs. The Reverend's door was ajar. As Johnnie crept by there was a bloodcurdling shriek.

"*Aaaaaaaaaaa*aaaaaaaaaa! The Wooooooolves! The Sheeeeeeeeeeeeeeeeeeep! The Sprockets are . . . aha! *Thwarted again! Eeeeeeeeeee*eeeeeeeeeeeeeeeeeeeeeeeee *eeeeeeeeeeeeee*eeeeeeeeeeeeeeeeeeeeeeeeee *Oh!*"

Johnnie froze. The skin on his back goose-pimpled. But a moment later he heard the quiet rasp of the Reverend's sleeping breath. Quickly he ran down the last flight of stairs and straight through the hall and down the corridor and into the kitchen, and drank three cups of cold, rusty water. He started to creep back toward the stairs, when he stopped stock-still.

In the hallway, propped against the radiator and surrounded by packages and dust sheets, was an extraordinary creature.

The windows had been left unshuttered, and moonlight glittered in on the massive figure. It was metal from head to foot. What struck Johnnie most of all was the *grin.* This grin was so broad and mad it seemed about to snap with its big teeth at whatever came near it. The one eye of the creature stared straight ahead, but the grin seemed to follow Johnnie as he walked around the object, examining it.

Greatly daring, he touched the metal leg with the tip of his finger, then gave it a little tap with his knuckle: Undoubtedly the thing was *hollow.* So it was only a dead machine. Strange, it had looked so real for a moment. Like a knight, or a giant. Just as a joke, Johnnie winked at it.

Very slowly, a silver shutter came down over the single eye and with a tiny clang flicked up again. Once more the creature stared straight ahead, as motionless as ever. Johnnie could see the barometer on the opposite wall mirrored in its eyeball.

He blinked at it several times, but it stared straight ahead.

"Oh, go on, you're nothing but an old tin toy," he whispered.

On the floor nearby was an Instruction Booklet and Operating Manual. Johnnie picked it up. The description in the opening paragraph made him go clammy. This was no toy—whoever heard of such a thing in Parchment House? No, this was a machine, a *robot*, brought in to torment and bully orphans.

Johnnie decided to try some sabotage before the Worthies had a chance to put it into operation. He began to pull haphazardly at some wires which hung out of a big power pack by the robot's feet, obviously waiting to be installed. He had pulled out a couple of wires when he received a tingling shock which made his veins fizz, his hair stand on end, and which lifted him two inches off the ground.

Without another glance at the robot, Johnnie streaked up the stairs, not caring whether he woke every Worthy in the place. He jumped straight into bed, snuggled down under the blankets, and lay there shivering, until the dawn started to turn the little window-circle cornflower blue.

4
ARCHIE LESSONS

For a few days no one paid any attention to the orphans. They were not summoned downstairs at all, but each morning some lukewarm soup and a plate of bread and cheese were left on a tray outside the attic door. Inky Dumb-Dumb would not eat anything at all, not even a crumb. He sat huddled in a corner. He frightened the younger children. After looking at him, Alice's face grew all blotchy as if she had measles, and she would go and lie under her bed for a while, in the dust, sucking her thumb.

Johnnie had told the others about the robot, but not about the wink. No one knew what to make of it all. They sat around the attic, waiting, but not knowing what they were waiting for. It was not so bad, being left alone for a while. But what was going on downstairs?

The Worthies were ignoring the children because they were busy trying to train the robot.

It looked a bit out of place among the furniture and machinery: Archibald was certainly a thing of bulk. Reverend Slipper had been studying the Manual. Now he was reading out instructions in a confident voice, as he did not want to betray the fact that he was a bit befuddled by the terminology. Mrs. Padlock sat fanning herself with a copy of *The Orphan Owners' Gazette*. Big Marvin sat slumped in a corner looking morosely at his feet in their battered tennis shoes.

Miss Stir, however, looked quite efficient, all dressed in brown overalls with an oily rag in the top pocket. Though all thumbs with delicate mechanisms, she was a whiz at anything more sturdy. With a few grunts of concentration, some joining of wires and checking of circuits, adjustments and tightening of bolts, she finally got to the point where only packaging was left on the floor: All the important elements were inserted into the robot.

The Reverend congratulated her. "Now let's get on with reading the Operating Manual. We shall see what happens."

Peering at the booklet, he began intoning, " '. . . and after checking all connections and deciding on instructions and giving aforesaid, press button marked START and retire to a safe distance to prepare for . . .' "

"Now, Reverend, that should be my contribution," said Mrs. Padlock, getting up from her armchair. She lunged at the button before anybody could stop her. For a moment nothing happened, then there was a rapid sparking from Archie's teeth; he rattled as if he was full of teaspoons, and then started to rock wildly from side to side. One of his great arms flailed in all directions, up, down, sideways, over and around and around and around, knocking some nearby trinkets into the air and catching Mrs. Padlock a stunning blow across the backside, which sent her flying across the room into the bookcase.

"Get up, get up, Mrs. Padlock. Miss Stir, would you please pass me the Operating Manual, which seems somehow to have got stuck under the robot's foot?"

Mrs. Padlock hobbled back to her armchair and sat there with her feet in their little boots lifted high off the carpet, as if she was afraid the robot was going to stamp on them.

Miss Stir, who had been bashed a couple of times by Archie but had taken it on the chin like a man, gave the robot a nonchalant shove, retrieved the Manual, threw it to the Reverend and, in almost the same gesture, pushed a button in the robot's back.

Immediately, all activity ceased. Archibald clanked to a stop and stood motionless, his arm slightly at an angle, but otherwise exactly as he had been before Mrs. Padlock's intervention.

Big Marvin, who had not moved from the corner, suddenly clapped his big hands three times on his knees and gave a great laugh.

"Are you laughing at *me*?" cried Mrs. Padlock in a fury, tapping at her wig, which had come a bit askew.

But big Marvin only yawned and went back to sleep.

"Really," said Mrs. Padlock, "the man is not fit to be a Worthy. You ought to write to the Authorities, Reverend, and get them to send a replacement."

Reverend Slipper shrugged. He did not want to think about big Marvin *at all.*

"Never mind, never mind. If you had not been so impulsively helpful, Mrs. Padlock, we would have got where we intended a good deal more quickly."

Miss Stir took the Manual from the Reverend.

"If I might speak. Let's try out some simple mechanical programs. Just talk into the machine's microphone and, provided you say the words clearly and in an approved language, it will carry out instructions until told to stop. Hang on . . . it gets a little more complicated. . . ." She turned the page, frowning. "It says here that 'since this is a Model the endless permutations have not been fully explored. A whole world of infinite possibilities opens before you.' Well, I think we ought to try and grasp all that later. The Basic Operating Procedure is what we should go on for the moment."

They cleared a space and, programing Archibald carefully, gradually managed to maneuver him around. After a long time, they at last managed to get the hang of controlling the great creature.

Mrs. Padlock said she would knit Archibald a Fair Isle sweater and tie, and would run up a pair of flannel trousers and a short-sleeved white shirt. She also agreed to knit some box-shaped gray socks. Shoes were obviously out of the question for such vast feet. They hoped the robot would not slip on the stairs. Miss Stir was put in charge of general mechanisms and Reverend Slipper elevated himself to the post of Chief Inventor of Programs and Organizer of Robotic Personnel. Nobody could think what role big Marvin could play so they gave him a can of metal polish and some dust cloths and hoped he would lend a hand. Big Marvin put these things under his bed and they were never seen again.

It was time to try the robot out on the orphans.

A gong boomed out through the building.

"It ain't a fire," said Solly Turk, "because them down there'd just leave us to fry. Them'd probably try to get insurance on us."

Again the gong boomed, and then Mrs. Padlock's voice came up the stairs. "Assemble in the schoolroom in an orderly fashion. Come on now, hurry up."

"Ugh," said Solly Turk, but he began to do up his shoelaces.

"Perhaps this is it," said Johnnie. "Perhaps now we'll know what kind of thing they've brought in to torment us."

The children left the attic and climbed down the stairs and hurried into the schoolroom.

Mrs. Padlock was now sitting on a chair by the blackboard, and Miss Stir was leaning against the wall with her hands in her pockets. The orphans sat down at their desks. There was silence, and then a clanking shuffle could be heard coming along the corridor.

Crash!

Archibald's head had hit the doorframe! With some difficulty the robot was at last maneuvered into the schoolroom. Reverend Slipper followed close behind. Archibald took up a position on the platform.

The children stared in amazement. The creature was *enormous*. It made them dizzy just to look at it. The metal plume on top of its head, which had been bent in the collision with the doorframe, had sprung back, and its tip brushed the ceiling.

Johnnie Rattle stared particularly at the robot's eye. But the great silver orb between the fringe of metal eyelashes was as blank as the top of a gatepost.

The Worthies gathered around the robot.

"Give him his stick, Mrs. Padlock," ordered Reverend Slipper.

She handed the robot a long bamboo cane with a prong screwed into the end. The robot immediately began to beat frenziedly on the desk.

"*Stop! Stop!* It is to be used on children, not on furniture!"

Archie looked as if he was prepared to beat *everyone* to smithereens.

"You really must behave with more circumspection," scolded Mrs. Padlock.

"It is not good talking to him—it—like that," said Miss Stir. "You have to say *stop* very firmly into the microphone, and if that doesn't work you have to push the STOP button in its back. But you must address him firmly. You have to think of the thing as a cross between a dog and a machine."

"*Sit,*" said Mrs. Padlock, firmly, to Archibald. With a tremendous clatter, the robot sat down, breaking the chair and knocking over the table at the same time. There was also a ripping sound as his trousers split. The plastic tulips, which had been sitting on top of the table for years and years, getting dustier and dustier, scattered in all directions. A few children snickered, but most of them went pale. The Worthies managed to haul Archibald back to his feet.

"Now, I'll ask the questions," said the Reverend, "and you can manipulate it to give the answers, Miss Stir. Then we can program it so that it asks the questions, and the orphans give the answers. Then we can arrange a system of rewards and punishments for correct or incorrect answers."

"What would the rewards be?" asked Mrs. Padlock, doubtfully.

"The rewards will be not to be punished," said Reverend Slipper.

"Oh, good, that's all right then."

33

Reverend Slipper took a sheet of paper out of his pocket.

"I find I have some jottings here. Now, what shall we choose to demonstrate to these orphans the immense learning of the robot? History geography physics French photography trigonometry biology ornithology or another subject of your own choice?"

"Orni what?" murmured Miss Stir.

"Where's big Marvin?" said Mrs. Padlock unexpectedly. "Big Marvin should be here to share this notable occasion."

"Big Marvin is busy shirking his duties as usual," said Reverend Slipper. "RIGHT, ARCHIBALD! A GEOGRAPHICAL QUESTION COMING UP! WHAT IS THE PRINCIPAL CROP OF BRAZIL?"

There was a whirring noise, and then the robot said in an expressionless, clipped growl, "Coffee toffee."

"Toffee as well? How very interesting."

"Ask him another."

"WHAT IS THE MAIN EXPORTABLE EDIBLE FOODSTUFF OF ITALY?"

"There's no need to shout," said Miss Stir.

Archie whirred again: "Yeti confetti libretti Donizetti Rosetti betty sweaty betty sweaty betty . . ."

"STOP. Try again. What is the main exportable edible foodstuff of Italy?"

"Dante chianti andante."

"He's ever so cultivated," said Mrs. Padlock.

"This is very interesting," said Reverend Slipper. "He obviously knows a great deal. Shall we try him on one more geographical question? Right. What is the principal need of all the natives of the Empire?"

All the Worthies knew the answer to this one: Missionary Orphans. They all waited expectantly as Archibald whirred once more.

34

"Slaughter daughter taught her caught her brought her fought her water water water water . . ."

Miss Stir jiggled Archibald's back mechanism a little and the Reverend asked the question again.

Archibald seemed to take a little longer this time.

At last he said: "Chilblain scatterbrain cellophane airplane champagne cocaine sugar cane hurricane porcelain . . ."

"Porcelain? Surely that can't be right. What would natives want with *porcelain*?"

". . . counterpane down the drain weather vane Tarzan and Jane pain pain the rain in Spain the rain the rain rain rain rain rain . . ."

The robot stopped speaking and whirring and stood there quite impassive.

The children stared at it open-mouthed, except for Alice, who hid under the desk, and Inky Dumb-Dumb, who was curled up in a heap as usual. The thin Twins twittered and rolled their big eyes. Jane Pegg made a kind of squeaking noise.

"Silence," cried Mrs. Padlock. She didn't know what to make of the robot's answers. They didn't sound like the answers she had been brought up with. But did that matter? After all, they were official, so to speak. Archibald was supposed to be the latest thing. Perhaps the answers had changed without her knowing it. It was a little difficult to keep up with the times in Carstairs and Bungho.

"Why not try him with some geometry?" asked Miss Stir.

Reverend Slipper knew nothing of geometry.

"After you, Miss Stir."

"Oh, all right. Archibald, listen now. To what is the square on the hypotenuse equal?"

The question had an electrifying effect. Instead of

picking up a piece of chalk and writing the answer on the blackboard, Archibald began to march all over the place, knocking down anything in his way, including Mrs. Padlock. Miss Stir realized he was making an attempt to demonstrate the theorem in actual space, but to the others he appeared to be giving a random example of a robot running amok. Miss Stir leaped for the STOP button.

Reverend Slipper was furious. He added to the shambles by seizing the bamboo cane and hitting out at random.

"BE QUIET!" he shouted at the top of his voice. He was determined to have one last try.

"History—we'll try him on the Kings and Queens of England. ARCHIBALD . . ."

"It's no use shouting. . . ."

"Archibald . . . What King of England had his head cut off?"

Archibald whirred busily. "Charles the First walked and talked half an hour after his head was cut off."

"Yes, well, spare us the gory details, but quite right in essence. Now, Mrs. Padlock, you have a turn."

"Who were the six wives of Henry the Eighth?"

"The Queen of Spain's daughter, Mary Mary, Ann Ann, and a frying pan."

"I don't think that's *quite* right. . . ."

"Oh, it'll do," said the Reverend hurriedly. After all, the orphans wouldn't have a clue who Henry the Eighth's wives were, so they'd be none the wiser. The thing was to get something, never mind what, into orphans' heads, in order to keep out all the other things that might get in there of their own accord if one didn't get there first.

"Ask him another, Mrs. Padlock."

Mrs. Padlock's history was hazy, but she thought she ought to have one more try.

"Who is the patron saint of England?"

"That's not about Kings and Queens."

"Hush, he's going to say something."

"Georgie Porgie Pudding and Pie," said the robot.

"And who or what did he have a famous fight with?"

The robot whirred for a long time.

"Lady Godiva's horse," he said at last, and fell backward, steaming slightly from the strain.

The first Archie Lesson was over.

5

A BIRD?

It was late that night. The orphans were asleep. All through their dreams the robot was stomping after them on its metal feet, its plume waving, its big eye gleaming. They twisted and whimpered in their sleep, trying to get away.

But Johnnie Rattle was lying staring into the dark. The whole day had been like a dream, but now that night had come he was suddenly wide awake. He got up, knelt on the bed, and gazed out toward the forest and the distant tower silhouetted against the sky. The moon had risen, a small brilliant moon that lit up the countryside and the garden with an eerie light. Down below, the side lawn, newly mown by Shambles, shone like silver. But as Johnnie looked at it a darkness started to spread over the grass, as if an underground stream had met an obstruction and had burst upward to inundate the lawn. The whole night seemed suddenly shadowed over. Johnnie looked up toward the sky.

An enormous bird with jagged wings was flying over Parchment House. Its head was bony, and it had a beak shaped like a pair of pruning shears, a ridged body, and a wedge-shaped tail that ended in a small black tendril. Slowly the bird moved across the sky, and its shadow moved in unison over the clipped lawn. Then the shadow bent slightly as it vanished over the countryside, and the dragonlike creature itself grew smaller and smaller until it looked like a bat over the distant forest.

Johnnie peered and peered until the shape was no more than a speck. Then the night sky was empty again, the moon shone as before, and nothing seemed to have changed.

He gripped the edge of the windowsill and blinked several times. The bird seemed to have left behind a kind of shadow on his retina, the reflection of a shadow, like the dark mark that hovers in front of you when you have been staring at a candle flame. It had been utterly silent, gliding past in the night and then vanishing into the darkness of the horizon. The creature had been like something made from floating stone, its eye seeming to be no more than a hole cut in its head through which the moonlight shone. Johnnie gazed out toward the forest as if he could summon it back.

For one moment, while the apparition had passed overhead, one jagged wing had seemed to touch the moon while the other brushed the chimneys of

Parchment House. And at that moment, a surge of power had jolted through the air, as if the bars and walls and locks of Parchment House had melted away, and Johnnie had felt he was free, floating out through the window and over the sky toward the forest like the bird.

But had it been a bird? Where had it come from? Sometimes old balloons and such things went drifting over Parchment House, advertising detergents, or a Peace and Unity Spiritualist Meeting in Carstairs's town hall. But this had been nothing of that kind. Had it been only a dream? Johnnie pinched the skin on his arm. That didn't feel like dreaming. What had happened? He looked around the cubicle. There was nothing in it except the bed, his ragged clothes, and the geranium. One of the red flowers had begun to wilt, and there were three petals on the floor, looking dark in the moonlight like drops of blood.

Carefully Johnnie picked them up and laid them on the curve of the windowsill, one in the middle and two slanted on each side. That was the nearest he could get to recreating the shape of a bird. Then he got back into bed and fell asleep at once.

When he woke the next morning the geranium petals were still on the windowsill, growing dark and wrinkled in the morning light. Johnnie did not tell anybody about the night bird. After a while he could hardly believe what he had seen himself.

6

ARCHIE FACTS

Since the first Archie Lesson had not gone completely without a hitch, the Worthies spent another week working on a rigorous training schedule for the robot. Archibald was not absolutely reliable on all counts. For instance, his carpentry was distinctly erratic. Nails got bent, and glue spread everywhere, so that Mrs. Padlock went about for a whole morning with a matchbox stuck to her backside, and could not work out why sitting down was so uncomfortable. Also, Archibald did not seem able to formulate questions on his own. He did, however, manage to produce a stream of Basic Facts, such as: the population of Peru the highest mountain in Nepal the site of the end of the rainbow the role of entropy in fortune-telling the mileage to Babylon as the crow flies and in modern transport terms various methods of cooking jam . . . An astonishing number of Facts! The Worthies were amazed! All, that is, except for big Marvin, who during the long training sessions was either absent or else sat slumped in the corner armchair gazing at the floor, sometimes with his eyes open and sometimes not. What a blot upon the proceedings! Mrs. Padlock itched to kick him with the sharp toe of her button boot. But something stopped her. She gave him a wide berth, having to content herself with mutterings and sighs in his direction, to which big Marvin paid no notice at all.

After much hard work in the front room, Archibald was taken outside for some military drill. The Reverend had a theory that to give orders one must know how to take orders, and the robot was certainly going to have to give some pretty firm orders in the future. So, Archibald was marched up and down, and created havoc among Shambles's carefully tended nettle beds and rows of beets and potatoes.

At last his training was complete. The Worthies decided to keep him in the laundry, as it was handy to the schoolroom. There was plenty of space in there, and no valuables, and he could be oiled every morning without getting grease all over the carpet. Besides, having him downstairs was damaging everything, and, in spite of the socks, his feet had made marks on the hall floor that were far worse than the little crescents left by Mrs. Padlock's boots. Mrs. Padlock herself sewed up Archibald's trousers with button thread and a double seam to make sure they did not split again.

Everything was organized. In the supremely important Control and Discipline Procedure, Archibald had proved to be a first-class recruit. It was time to unleash him on the orphans once again.

The gong rang. The orphans gathered in the schoolroom. The robot entered, marching confidently with a military clang. Johnnie stared at the creature. Not a wink, not a tremor, softened the terrible grin. The one eye stared straight ahead. The right hand was clenched around the big cane.

Reverend Slipper read out some instructions, then pressed the START button. The robot clicked two or three times and then began to speak in a mechanical drone. Facts began to issue from between the clenched teeth.

"You are to copy everything down in the notebooks provided," said the Reverend. *"Everything."*

He listened for a few minutes to Archibald's monologue, then went out, smiling to himself, leaving the robot alone in charge of the orphans. They wrote and wrote. Pen points broke and pencils were worn down to stubs. Page after page was filled, but still the Facts came pouring forth. The orphans couldn't make head or tail of the whole thing.

Tiggy got in a panic and threw her notebook on the floor and started to growl and scream. "I'm not a-going to, I'm not. I'm not. Go on, go on, ye canna mek me do it!" But in a moment, the robot had crossed the room, knocking over desks and children in the process, and had clanked down on Tiggy like a heap of scrap metal. It grabbed her tangled hair and thumped her head down several times on the desk, before administering a series of thwacks which turned the girl into a terrified statue. When Jackie and Grub began to wail, the robot turned on its axis so swiftly they stopped in mid-cry and

43

just stared at it open-mouthed, too frightened to blink, even. Archibald stood motionless for a second, whining softly; then his mechanism gave a lurch and he marched back to the platform, stepping over, without touching, the form of Inky Dumb-Dumb prostrate on the floor.

Once more the Facts started to pour from the robot's grinning mouth. Tiggy picked up her notebook and wrote through a mush of tears that dropped on the book and made the ink run. Still she went on writing, blindly, not understanding a word.

The lessons continued day after day. Sometimes the robot drew weird diagrams on the blackboard, or even on the floor, a whirring sound coming from the back of its neck. Sometimes it clanked its arms about as if it was conducting an orchestra. But most of the time it just stood there, pouring forth hours of gibberish which the children tried vainly to copy down. They were going through several notebooks a week. The Reverend put in an order for extra stationery, and looked with satisfaction at the piles of Archie Facts that were collecting in the school cupboard. There would certainly be plenty to show the Governors when they came on their Annual Visit at the end of the summer.

The children were bruised all over, as Archibald reacted violently to every squeak or wriggle or cough. Throughout the day their heads buzzed with the drone of his voice, and at night it went on through their dreams. They looked even grayer and iller than usual. Alice's hair started falling out in tufts, and her face grew blotchier and blotchier so that she looked like a mildewed strawberry.

Only Inky Dumb-Dumb seemed unaffected by Archibald but still crouched in the corner with his head hidden in his rags. The robot seemed to pay no attention to Inky Dumb-Dumb either, as if the child did not really exist. But the others were worn to a frazzle by the thing, and they still had all the work with the gadgets to deal with after the daily Archie Lesson. They walked about in a daze, too miserable even to feel hungry, except for Grub, who was *always* hungry.

Day after day the torment went on.

Johnnie Rattle felt a rage against the robot growing inside him day by day. He closed his mind against the drone of Facts and wrote mumbo jumbo of his own. If Archibald thwacked him he tried not to flinch. He stared at the robot as once he had stared at Reverend Slipper.

"I shall *get* you, Archibald. You won't get me!"

Mrs. Padlock and Reverend Slipper were agog with energy. Mrs. Padlock spent her time poring over holiday brochures, and Reverend Slipper had many happy hours with his air gun. It was true what the flier had said:

ARCHIE CAN DO ANYTHING YOU CAN DO AND MORE MORE MORE LEAVING YOU ALL THAT TIME TO DO ALL THE THINGS YOU'VE ALWAYS WANTED TO DO BUT NEVER THOUGHT YOU COULD!

The Reverend had half a mind to write to the Authorities about the amazing creature that had been acquired by Parchment House, which was capable of running an entire orphanage almost single-handed. But then he had a thought—if Archibald's efficiency was bragged about too widely, it might be thought that a small robot platoon could render obsolete a whole host of charitable schoolteachers. Instead of having a holiday in Blackpool they might all end up trudging to the unemployment office in Carstairs and Bungho, and might even, in due course, be cast out of town. No, no—better to keep the matter dark!

He decided instead to write to the Useful Machine

Factory (Robots) Ltd. to find out the state of things as far as other robots were concerned. He got a letter back saying that the former Useful Machine Factory (Robots) Ltd. was now simply called the Useful Machine Factory, and was no longer interested in manufacturing Archibalds. The expense involved in setting up the model had not been justified as regards the level of interest shown by the public.

Reverend Slipper heaved a sigh of relief: Archibalds would not be taking over the entire teaching profession. But then he realized something. Archibald was not merely a model—he was unique! That meant he was extremely valuable! Suppose somebody heard about the robot's wonderful exploits and decided to steal it?

The Reverend wrote again to the Useful Machine Factory, and asked them if they manufactured burglar alarms. But they wrote back saying no, they had gone into video machines which recorded your own life and played it back to you complete, thus eliminating any need on your part to exert yourself the day after the recording, as you could spend the twenty-four hours of that day watching what you had been doing during the twenty-four hours of the previous day. It was suggested that this regime, if followed indefinitely and without interruption, might produce dwindling returns, but the project had spectacular if limited potential for the leisure hours you like to spend with your family and so on. Could they interest him, *Reverend Slipper* of *Parchment House*, a valued customer, in the purchase of such a machine?

Reverend Slipper threw this rubbish into his Automange basket and went to look for Shambles. He found him sitting on the compost heap having a quiet smoke.

"Would you be capable of rigging up an anti-theft

device to protect the robot at night?"

"I might and I mightn't. Have you asked Miss Stir? I might give it a try if she lent a hand."

Miss Stir was quite agreeable to this suggestion, and she and Shambles managed to rig up a system which protected Archibald while he stood in the laundry room at night. They even incorporated a special anti-rust gadget, which also worked as mechanism cleaner and power booster, so that Archibald could be cleaning himself and renewing his energies all night long. Shambles and Miss Stir did not argue as much as might have been expected. The work was soon done. Miss Stir was rather proud of the contraption.

Reverend Slipper slept well the night the alarm was fitted. He had a dream which made his sleepy face twitch nastily: rows of blue-gray orphans were marching around and around in a stone yard, while the sun beat down upon them. Suddenly a great shape dived down out of the sky. It picked up the blue-gray shape that was Johnnie Rattle and flew seaward, the scruff of Johnnie's neck caught in its big beak, the rest of the boy's body dangling like a rag doll. Wings beat powerfully through the Reverend's sleep; a peaceful shadow spread across his brain. A sweet dream indeed.

7

THE WORTHIES' ROOMS

At night, Parchment House is dark. Everyone—almost everyone—is sleeping. Reverend Slipper is sleeping in his grim, plain room. The walls of this room are covered with stern mementos: the head of a stuffed hyena; a snapshot of the Reverend's mother in a woolly coat and earmuffs; a picture of a goat and a copy of a diploma from the School of Moral Studies in Eastern England. There are also some brownish watercolors, given to the Reverend by Mrs. Padlock, depicting village scenes in the Hindu Kush, and a souvenir shield, decorated with crossed canes and a skull, donated to the orphanage by grateful natives at the Correction School in Balyhoo Bala.

There are few gadgets in this room—only the Ablution Machine in the corner, and, on a shelf nearby, the Worship Transistor, a device which will, at the press of a button, emit homilies and hymns for every day of the year. Next to the Transistor is a long black box. Inside this box is the Reverend's cut-throat razor.

Against one wall is the Reverend's cupboard, in which hang the Reverend's clothes, gray, black, and fawn, all giving off that chemical smell peculiar to the Reverend.

And here is Reverend Slipper himself, sleeping on his narrow bed, under two gray blankets and a thin gray sheet. His head is on a hard bolster. He sleeps with his teeth bared in a wolfish grin.

Just down the corridor sleeps Mrs. Padlock in her jumbled room. Though she is forever fidgeting about, trying to straighten out this room, her tidying consists of moving piles of things from one place to another, which is already full of things and which, in their turn, need to be piled up and moved elsewhere. Mrs. Padlock's room smells like the back of a food cupboard; that part where all the gravy mix and dried-up sauces, the little bottles of almond and peppermint extract, the cheese crumbs, old jam jars, and rusty soup cans get forgotten about. The smells of all these things amalgamate into one smell, and that is what Mrs. Padlock's room smells like.

Mrs. Padlock is lying asleep in her old bed, beneath the heavy bedspread, the seven blankets, and the pink sheet. Underneath Mrs. Padlock is another pink sheet, the electric blanket, and the Keepuwarmheat-reflector.

Mrs. Padlock is rather hot. She is dripping with sweat. She is dreaming, tonight, of orphans. What are the orphans doing? They are wading in a beautiful river they are floating away down a beautiful river and the river is full of crocodiles and on the other bank a host of angels is singing and it is all very beautiful. Mrs. Padlock snuffles in her sleep. She is content.

Miss Stir has a room like a cell. All here is gray and brown. Miss Stir's bed is the other half of the Reverend's divan set. Miss Stir lies in it as straight and as stiff as the effigy on a crusader's tomb. She does not have dreams, or at least any that she can remember, but falls into sleep like a diver entering a deep lake. She does not surface until early dawn when, with a start, she is suddenly awake and ready to go.

Her room is full of manuals: car manuals; electricity manuals; *How To Make It Work With Magnets; Anesthetics for the Amateur; Great Motorcycles of the World; 101 Things To Make With Old Bottles.* They are piled everywhere, and go back years in some cases, though no one has ever seen Miss Stir purchasing such things. Miss Stir's room is also full of bottles of turpentine substitute, cans of paint, screwdrivers, and oil cans. On a peg hangs her gravy-colored bathrobe. Miss Stir does not have an Ablution Machine, as she prefers to wash downstairs at the rain barrel just outside the back door, using cold water and a washcloth. That is why there is a rim of gray right around the edge of Miss Stir's neck—the bit that is just hidden by the collars of her gray check shirts.

No one can get into big Marvin's room except for big Marvin. He carries the only key in his pocket. No light shines beneath the door or through the keyhole, because the inside of the door is hung with a thick black curtain. Beyond is a room the like of which is not seen elsewhere at Parchment House. It is a smoky place, lit by candles. They stand everywhere, fixed on to white saucers, their reflections fluttering in the narrow mirrors that hang all around the room, and in the big round mirror that hangs above the fireplace, its bulging surface distorting everything that shines across it. There is another light that seems to come and go through this room in surges, so that sometimes the air whitens and sharpens as if lit up by a flare, and then the air dims, and there is a strong smell of marshes and fogs. Then it settles down to candlelight again.

On the walls, between the mirrors, is a honeycomb of shelves, stocked with a hodgepodge of things. For example: a white twiggy tree in a goldfish bowl; a glowing blob in a pickle jar; lumps of coal; carved stone pyramids; ropes, ribbons, and iron tools. There are also some dog-eared books, several old socks, and an empty beer bottle covered with dust and labeled "Pig and Firework Best Home Brew."

A big fire crackles and hisses in the hearth. Nearby, on the floor, is a kingfisher in a glass case.

Big Marvin's bed fills up the whole of the center of the room, but it is almost invisible beneath the heap of cloth which is piled up on it like clothes on a rummage sale stall. There are pieces of blue cloth embroidered with gold, and black cloth, and lengths of a gauzy fabric which seems to be made out of the pulverized wings of dragonflies. Mixed up with all this cloth are other things—shards of mirror glass, a flute, some nails, a thermometer. Also some sooty tongs.

Big Marvin is not sleeping under all this cloth. He is, for once, wide awake, and is pottering about barefoot among a whole collection of test tubes, glass rods, and buckets that clutters up the space in front of the fire.

Over his crumpled suit he is wearing a most curious garment, which makes him resemble an exotic bag lady, a garment made out of bits of things—strips of leather, feathers, tassels, pieces of glass, pieces of embroidery, shells, bones, and little bells, all tied together with what looks like a lot of shoelaces. On his head, big Marvin wears a big, wide-brimmed hat.

He picks a nail out of a jam jar and bangs his teeth with it, looking thoughtful. Now that big Marvin's eyes are, unusually, open, it can be seen that they are extremely curious eyes for a person, and would really be better suited to an owl. They are of a strange gold color, with a pupil like a big speck of soot. Big Marvin bangs his teeth and stares at the air. Then he throws the nail back into the jam jar and crosses the room to where a half-finished tapestry leans against the far wall. He stares at the tapestry. What does it represent? There is a lot of green thread. In the middle is a kind of column, and what looks like a yellow bird on top. Big Marvin stands before the thing. In the flickering light the threads seem suddenly to twist together and shake themselves for a moment into a forest, with real leaves. Big Marvin gives a great laugh which makes the candles flex their long flames, then he picks up the needle and begins to sew more green stitches into the big frame.

8

REBELLION

After a few weeks of Archie Lessons, the orphans had reached the limit of their endurance. Johnnie Rattle and Solly Turk had had enough. Late at night they sat in Johnnie's cubicle discussing the robot. Even though they were talking in undertones, Percival could hear them. The fat boy was sitting in bed, eating a toffee bar which was covered with fluff from having been stored, half-licked, under his pillow. Percival's eyes widened—they were plotting against the robot! What could they be thinking of! He listened more closely: "Tools . . . rubbish . . . Facts . . . midnight . . . get it when it's off-guard . . . sabotage . . . mechanism . . . destroy it before it . . . demolition job . . . " Percival leaned even nearer to the cubicle curtains to hear the details more clearly, and dropped his toffee bar onto the floor. It got all covered with fluff from the carpet to add to the fluff from under the pillow. His cross squeal produced a sudden silence from the next cubicle. Then Percival heard Solly creep back to his own space.

Johnnie Rattle did not sleep immediately. He knelt on his bed and looked out through the round window toward the forest. There seemed to be a light coming from the top of the tower, winking on and off, but always at the edge of sight. When he looked directly at the place it seemed to come from, there was darkness.

All around him he could feel the bulk of Parchment House, the dour rooms where nothing happened, where all an orphan had to live on was lies and bullying and nettle soup, where an orphan was punished for nothing at all and was shut up away from the sun for years and years on end. Johnnie gritted his teeth in the darkness and banged his fist on the old blankets. Why *should* he be thumped and bullied by a great metal giant with no brains at all?

Underneath his mattress he had a secret cache of tools. They had been collected, one by one, during gadget mending, then hidden under his shirt and sneaked up here. They were for when the time came for attacking Archibald.

"You just wait, you bullying monster," muttered Johnnie. "You just wait. I'll get you one of these days! You're only another gadget, and I know how to deal with *them!*"

The tower and the forest were black. It had grown cold. Johnnie shivered and got into bed. But for a long time he could not sleep. Archibald seemed to be clanking through his mind, the big eye staring, the teeth clenched in that terrible grin.

On Sundays, Archibald was put in storage for twenty-four hours. Out of the cupboard in the schoolroom were brought old iron chairs, on which the children had to sit from dawn to dusk, in a semicircle in the front of the schoolroom, while Hymns of Empire were played on the old gramophone. The gramophone was operated by an orphan winding a handle around and around nonstop.

It was here, sitting on one of these iron chairs, listening to "The Sun Never Sets on Hideyhangoo," that Johnnie decided the time had come to launch an attack on Archibald. He thought back to his first sight of the robot: That wink in the hall must have been a trick of the moonlight. Archibald was nothing but a lifeless monster. There was nothing to do but destroy the thing. "Tonight's going to be the night!" said Johnnie to himself.

The Worthies were downstairs relaxing. Every now and then Reverend Slipper or Mrs. Padlock would put their heads around the door to check that everyone was sitting still. Alice, who had been turning the gramophone handle for a long time, had sweat dripping into her eyes, and she was crying because her arm hurt after so much effort. Reverend Slipper peered around the door and, seeing her tiring, ran in and beat her over the head with a hymn book, crying, "On, on, forever onward, be mindful of the welfare of the Heathen. Remember those to whom you owe allegiance. Be grateful. Think of your sins. Repent. On, ever onward."

Alice collapsed on the floor and said she could not go ever onward for another minute.

"No supper for you, weakling," hissed the Reverend, tweaking her ear. He looked about for a substitute orphan to wind the gramophone.

"You," he said, pointing at Inky Dumb-Dumb.

The children murmured.

"Silence!"

Inky Dumb-Dumb crawled toward the gramophone.

"Get on with it!" shouted Reverend Slipper, belaboring him with the hymn book.

Inky put out a clawlike hand and slowly turned the handle. The noise that came out was like an old door creaking open.

"Faster!"

The creaking noise went on. Inky Dumb-Dumb tottered.

"Faster! Faster!"

Johnnie Rattle sprang to his feet.

"I'll work the gramophone!"

Reverend Slipper's face twitched with annoyance. But the awful grinding noise coming out of the gramophone was never going to fill the orphans with a sense of missionary zeal.

"Very well, Johnnie Rattle. Make sure you do not falter. I shall be back to check."

Johnnie came up and obediently began to turn the handle. Reverend Slipper looked at him suspiciously, but Johnnie kept his head down. The Reverend went out.

Johnnie turned the handle around and around. If anyone stopped turning, the music crackled on for a moment and then the machine started running down. Around and around, on and on, Johnnie turned the handle. He started to laugh, silently, inside himself. The laugh started in his belly and spread. Furiously he turned and turned. Archibald, he thought, you're first on the list. The laugh spread to the roots of his hair and to his fingertips. Away with Reverend Slipper! Down the hatch with Mrs. Padlock! Off with the lot of you! I'll give you Hymns of Empire, I will!

The other children were starting to laugh too, out loud. Without realizing it, Johnnie's vigorous turning had knocked the handle slightly off kilter. It had started to turn faster and faster, so that the massed voices singing the chorus of "We Shall Bring Them Sunshine Where Darkness Reigned E'er Now," which up till then had been giving a dreary version of the old favorite, at first hesitantly and then at full tilt, started to shriek quicker and quicker until they were singing in a jumbled squeal that seemed to fall over itself. Johnnie turned the volume as high as it would go. The orphans started shrieking with the record and banging their heels on the floor. A couple of iron chairs fell over with a tremendous crash. The orphans began to clap their hands, and then to riot around the schoolroom.

Reverend Slipper and Mrs. Padlock came rushing in. The pandemonium struck them dumb for a moment. Johnnie looked up with glittering eyes and continued to turn the handle. Reverend Slipper launched himself at the boy and, tearing him from the gramophone, hurled him across the room. Johnnie skidded into the wall. A map of the Empire fell off its hook. Suddenly the schoolroom was so quiet you could have heard a mouse cleaning its whiskers.

The Reverend said in a voice of cold fury, "Water and crumbs only, and all belongings to be confiscated forthwith and forever."

The children were banished to their cubicles. They lay there in silent terror. Nothing happened for a long time, but then, just when they were dropping off to sleep, Mrs. Padlock burst in carrying a large flashlight and an enormous black garbage bag. Her face was bloated with excitement. She stormed through the cubicles, seizing everything she could find, every fragment of glass and bone and scrap of wool—even Jackie Daw's magic stone, which he had hidden at the bottom of his bed.

His cries were terrible to hear.

Johnnie was just reaching out to hide the geranium under his bed when he felt Mrs. Padlock's hand grab the hair at the back of his neck.

"No you don't! Give that here!"

"I will not!"

In the struggle between them, the geranium tumbled to the floor. It fell out of the pot, spilling earth over the boards. Mrs. Padlock picked up the plant by its thick stem.

"Aha! What have we here? A little horticulturalist? Oho! We don't need flowers like this in Parchment House. What a scrubby little thing! To think we've got all those gladioli and daffodils in flexiplastic downstairs, and the little boy keeps this all to himself. Shall we take this down to the Reverend and ask him if he'd like a flower for his buttonhole? No, I know what we'll do!"

She snapped off the plant, so that she was left holding the flowers and leaves, while the root and stump fell to the floor. Then, she bit off the red flowers and wolfed them down.

"My, that was nice!"

One petal adhered to her lip like a drop of blood. Her horrible purple tongue came out and licked it in. She rolled her eyes.

"Delicious, a real delicacy . . . *Now* . . ." Suddenly she was glaring again. "*Now,* lie down and not a squeak out of you till morning."

58

She picked up the flashlight and the black garbage bag, which had fallen to the floor in the struggle, and stomped off through the attic.

Johnnie lay in bed, crying. When Mrs. Padlock had gone, he leaned out and picked up the stubby remains of his plant and, putting it gently back in the pot, set it on the floor beside him. The darkness grew thicker. Owls started hooting far off from the fields at the edge of the forest. Parchment House was silent.

Underneath the mattress were a hammer, some files, and a saw. He felt beneath the mattress for the cold metal, hauled out the tools, and put them in his filthy pillowcase. Then he crept out of bed, taking care not to wake the others, and ran stealthily on tiptoe down the space between the cubicles, out the door, and down the stairs.

Percival Amalgam, who was not asleep because of indigestion, heard the creaking floorboard at the top of the stairs. He lumbered out of bed and, keeping well out of sight, crept after Johnnie through the silent house.

Johnnie reached the laundry door. He fiddled expertly with the lock and soon felt it give. Slowly, slowly, he turned the handle. He gave the door a gentle push. It started to open. . . .

With a clanging that seemed to shake the dust out of the shadows, the burglar alarm sounded through the night.

Miss Stir stirred in her bed. "It works, it works, it works!"

Reverend Slipper rose from his divan with a great leap and, clad in his burlap pajamas, strode to the laundry room, grinding his teeth.

There was nobody there. The door was ajar, but

59

only to the width of the edge of a ruler. The Reverend pushed the door and switched off the alarm bell, then switched on the light. Archibald was exactly where he had been left on Saturday night, standing upright in the corner by the washing machine, grinning madly as usual. Reverend Slipper marched out of the room and caught sight of a figure lurking in the shadows. He seized the creature.

"Percival! What are you doing here?"

Percival was all aquiver. He could hardly breathe and his words were so high and jumbled that the Reverend could hardly understand a word he was saying, but eventually grasped that Johnnie Rattle . . .

"Johnnie Rattle! I might have guessed!"

Percival squeaked and gasped—Johnnie Rattle had been plotting against the robot . . . he didn't quite know . . . you see, he'd dropped his toffee and . . . and . . .

"Toffee? What toffee?" asked the Reverend in bewilderment.

"Coffeetoffee," said Archibald from the laundry room, but no one heard him.

Percival burbled on, but Reverend Slipper had understood enough. He bounded up the stairs to the attic. It was quiet. Nothing could be heard except the faintest un-sound of held breath. Reverend Slipper could feel the alertness of twelve pairs of eyes peering out into the darkness.

He marched into Johnnie's cubicle and pulled the boy from his bed. The pillowcase full of tools fell to the floor.

"Caught in the act!" shouted the Reverend.

He dragged the child to Mrs. Padlock's room. Mrs. Padlock was sitting in a bedraggled state, her sleeping wig askew over one eye, and the bedclothes bunched all around her so that she looked like an old bird in a nest.

"Summon the other Worthies! A massive crime has been committed!"

Big Marvin declined to be summoned, but Miss Stir came blundering along in her striped pajamas.

They all gazed at Johnnie while the Reverend explained the charges against him.

"Has no one any suggestion as to what we can do to punish this *vandal,* this *serpent?*"

"Send him to the farthest outpost of Empire by the next banana boat!" said Mrs. Padlock.

"My mind's a blank at this hour," said Miss Stir gruffly, looking uneasily at Johnnie.

"Look at him—orphan, hooligan, sniveler, *ingrate!* Scum of the earth! Brought from off the streets, torn from an inevitable life of crime, taken from the bosom of wickedness by our tender hands and kept in moral custody, and this is how he repays us! What have you got to say for yourself, boy?"

Johnnie Rattle stared at the Reverend and said nothing.

Mrs. Padlock looked with haughty distaste at Johnnie. That insolent stare! Her fingers itched to poke his eyes out. And then she had a brain wave!

"Get Archibald to deal with him!"

"Archibald? How could he help in this matter?"

"Let Archibald punish him. We needn't make ourselves responsible for what happens, need we? After all, this little fiend was prepared to vandalize the robot. Well then, fit the punishment to the crime. Shut him up for the rest of the night with the robot. Program it to 'punish' the child, but not to crush it to pieces, as we might have trouble with the Authorities when we come to collate the records if there's a whole child missing."

The Reverend could not understand how somebody

61

as dense as Mrs. Padlock could have come up with an idea of such brilliance. Only Miss Stir looked a little uneasy.

"Couldn't you think of something a little less drastic?" she said. "After all, our burglar alarm saved Archibald from any serious harm. I just feel you can't tell what a robot might do once it gets into uncharted territory. 'Punish' is a bit vague as a word. I can't help feeling that letting such a large creature turn the battery of its attention on a single child is rather a dangerous idea."

"Nonsense!" said the Reverend brusquely. "It's a simply wonderful idea. Well done, Mrs. Padlock."

He glared at Johnnie. He would have liked the child to get down on his knees and plead for mercy. But Johnnie just glared back. His face was gray, there were shadows under his eyes, but he did not look in the least as if he was going to beg for mercy.

"Take him by the ear, Mrs. Padlock, lest he try to escape his fate. So . . . to the laundry room!"

9
A NIGHT OF TRIAL

Johnnie was locked in the laundry room with Archibald.

The robot had been programed to

DEAL WITH THE INTRUDER WITHIN THE PARAMETERS OF THE INTRUDER'S SURVIVAL BUT OTHERWISE NO HOLDS BARRED.

Reverend Slipper had taken the bulb out of the light socket. The little red eye that showed that the washing machine was still plugged in glowed in the corner. The cold tap was dripping. Johnnie crouched against the wall. He felt light-headed, as if this was not happening to him. Archibald stood by the washing machine. A curious humming came from the robot, as if it was full of insects.

Johnnie stayed very still. But the robot began to move. Slowly the bulky creature shuffled toward him, closer and closer, until it was right up against him; he could smell its smell of metal polish and oil. He didn't dare look up, but stared at the big, boxy feet just in front of his own bare feet.

Suddenly the great hand came down and, before he knew what was happening, Johnnie was whirled up into the air and shaken backward and forward, up and down, as if he were a rat held in a cat's mouth. His teeth clattered together. He felt as if his brains were going to fall out. Then, just before he thought he was going to disintegrate completely, the robot hurled him from high up near the ceiling—*bang*—down on to the linoleum.

For a moment, Johnnie could not move. As he lay there the robot lifted its foot over his head and started to bring it slowly down; but just before it began to squash him flat, the foot stopped in midair, and Johnnie managed to summon up enough strength to roll away.

For a short while the robot stayed like that, one foot off the ground, unmoving. Scarcely daring to breathe, Johnnie lay stretched out on the linoleum, playing dead. It was no good, however. Eventually the robot shuddered, clomped its foot down on the floor, then reached over and seized the boy around the neck. Johnnie wanted to cry out, but the grip was too tight. The metal bit into his windpipe. Archibald clanked across the room, dragging Johnnie over the floor, and suddenly he found he was being shoved willy-nilly into the washing machine. It was a big industrial machine, but

Archibald had to push and push to get him into such a cramped space. Then the robot slammed shut the door. Johnnie's face was crushed against his knees. The top of the machine weighed down against the top of his head.

There was a far-off click, and cold water started seeping through the holes in the side of the drum. Slowly it began to fill, higher and higher, until water was lapping against Johnnie's cheek. He could make no noise. All he could hear was water trickling in and a kind of booming in his ears. Higher and higher the water rose. It bubbled into his mouth, then it splashed up his nostrils. Suddenly the water stopped rising. There was a moment when nothing happened, then the whole machine began to shudder and then to rock from side to side. Johnnie was jiggled about so his chin banged up and down on his knees and he bit his tongue. Then the shaking stopped and a dribble of water started to trickle in again. Johnnie felt as if his head was going to burst.

The water stopped again. There was a long pause. Then, as if from far-off and yet close-by, he heard a lot of clicking. The robot was fiddling with the controls. More noise of water—but this time it was draining away!

Nearly all the water was gone. Johnnie, sodden all over, still crouched there, his face crushed against his knees. A rumbling started. Once more the machine started to rock from side to side. Then the barrel began to whirl around and around, and Johnnie realized he was being spun like a wet sheet. Faster and faster the barrel whirled. All thoughts started to blow out of Johnnie's head. The feeling was almost peaceful, as if at any moment he would be propelled off, through the roof, toward the stars. But just as he was beginning to feel like a spaceman, or a bird, the machine lurched to a stop with a bang.

The door opened. A metal hand came in and grabbed Johnnie by the scruff of the neck. He was hauled back into the laundry room. After the dark inside the machine, the laundry seemed quite light. The robot held Johnnie close to its one eye and stared, then dropped him again with a big thump. Johnnie felt a sudden surge of anger.

"Leave me alone, you bully! Leave me alone!"

He pounded Archibald with his fists, but all he did was bruise his knuckles on the great metal body. He ran across to the window and tore at the catch, but it was locked. The robot clanked across and seized him again; the big fists started squeezing and squeezing. The metal felt as sharp as knives. But just as Johnnie thought the two halves of his body were going to be severed from each other, the robot relaxed its grip. Johnnie managed to snatch his breath before the terrible squeezing began again. Oh, stop stop! he cried inside, though he could not utter a word.

Suddenly the robot stopped squeezing altogether, and its humming turned into a kind of whine. It held Johnnie up close to its eye once more. Johnnie stared into the great metal orb. Everything seemed so bad, so hopeless, there was no longer any point in being afraid.

"You can do what you like with me," he said to Archibald, "only I'm not going to be scared of you any-more. You can squeeze me into little bits, or stamp on me, or grind me down into powder. I'm not going to utter one squeak or howl, not even inside myself. Only don't," he glared at the eye, "*don't* put me back in that washing machine. Do you hear? Do you understand, you dead, brainless, bullying old box, *do you hear?*"

The robot shuddered. Johnnie could feel a shock run right through it. He stared and stared into the robot's eye as if he was trying to hypnotize it into understanding him. The eye was a swiveling ball set in a circle, with a metallic fringe on the crescent lid, all set upon a short stalk. Suddenly, Johnnie became aware of something odd. Right in the middle of the ball a light was glowing. It was a light that was almost not a light. The harder he stared the more it seemed to disappear; but when he screwed up his own eyes and concentrated so hard he could *not* concentrate any harder, he saw it distinctly: a tiny brightness, right on the inside of the metal, which itself seemed to have become translucent.

Johnnie slowly reached out his hand and touched the eye.

He nearly squealed. Instead of being cold and metallic, the thing was warm and slippery, like a real eyeball. He smoothed his finger gently over the surface. As he did so, a kind of shiver went through the robot and, staring hard, Johnnie could just make out, deep inside the eye, a tiny furnace full of peacock green and gold and red flames which wove in and out of each other, giving off showers of sparks like fireworks. It was like looking at a place far far away—a garden, or a forest made of fire. For a moment he forgot all about the laundry and the robot and about Parchment House, and stared spellbound into the tiny nest of flames.

When he lifted his finger off the eyeball it stopped glowing and the light faded back to a pinpoint, though it was still there. The robot gave a snort. Then it suddenly put Johnnie down, fairly carelessly, but without violence.

"Ho, ho, ho!"

The robot sat down on the linoleum beside Johnnie.

"Ho, ho, ho!"

The noise was rather like a dog sneezing.

Johnnie thought: Well, the thing has gone really crazy now. He wondered about the STOP button on the back of the robot. Why had he not thought of that before? But as if it could read his mind, the robot shuffled around so that the button could not be reached. It hadn't completely lost its wits, then.

Johnnie watched Archibald. The sky was lightening, so he could see clearer every minute. The robot started picking off all the clothes that Mrs. Padlock had so carefully made for it. Off came the flannel trousers, and the socks, and the Fair Isle sweater, and the shirt—and there, at last, was the unadorned Archibald.

"You look better like that."

There was no reaction from the robot, which just sat there, clinking slightly. The whining inside it grew quieter and quieter, then suddenly stopped. Beyond the plink plink plink of the dripping tap Johnnie heard a night bird cry outside far far off, a long

WHOOOOO OOO WHOOOOOOOOooooooo . . .

The bird seemed to answer Archibald's snorty laugh with its melancholic hoot as it flew away over the fields. Johnnie listened to the sound fading into the night. He was tired to his bones and he hurt all over, but at least he was still in one piece. And it didn't look as if Archibald was going to cause any more trouble on this particular night. Stretching out on the floor, Johnnie fell fast asleep, and beside him, all of a heap, sat the robot.

They were found thus by the Worthies in the morning.

10

WHAT HAPPENED TO PERCIVAL?

Johnnie Rattle was carried to his cubicle by Shambles and Miss Stir. "Leave him there until he comes to his senses," were the Reverend's instructions. Miss Stir covered the boy with the old blankets and went away, but the next morning she climbed to the attic with a mug of soup, a glass of water, and some cheese on a cracked saucer, and laid them beside the bed where Johnnie still lay without moving. In the evening she took them away, the soup cold with a layer of grease on top, the cheese grown hard and sweaty. On the second day the same thing happened, only this time, when the sound of Miss Stir's hobnailed boots was heard on the stairs in the evening, Philadelphia snatched the cheese and hid it under her mattress, to be shared out later.

Still Johnnie did not move. His face was gray, as if he were made out of stone. The orphans kept very quiet. Every now and then one of them peered around the curtains, then crept away, too scared to say a word. Even Grub and Tiggy and Jackie scarcely dared to whisper, though Tiggy still growled in her sleep.

And then at last, when there was no one else in the attic, Johnnie opened his eyes. It was a warm day. A spider was crawling across the sloping ceiling above his bed. Downstairs he could hear a voice, but too far away to make out whose. He lay very still, watching the spider. Then he became aware of the sound of soft steps and then the sound of someone breathing close by. A face was looking at him around the edge of the cubicle curtains. The face vanished. A few minutes later Anna, Jackie, and Solly Turk crowded into the cubicle.

"What happened? Tell us! You've been lying here for *days!*"

"I had a fight with the robot."

"Who won, who won?"

Johnnie took a sip of water.

"I don't know. It wasn't that kind of fight. I don't want to talk about it. I don't want to think about it. Not yet. It's too strange to think about." Johnnie shook his head, which still felt muzzy. "What I want to know is, what's been happening while I've been asleep?"

"Well," said Solly Turk, "we got Percival! Because it was him snitched on you. The fat pig came in here after that noise woke us all up. We was all sitting up in bed. 'What you been doing, Percival?' we said, because we knew the Rev had gone and grabbed you and we thought Percival had something to do with it as we'd heard him sneaking downstairs all excited like. For a bit he wouldn't tell us and then he started strutting about with that waddle of his, and then he said he'd been saving the robot! 'The nice robot!' *That's* what he called it. A reward, that's what he wanted! From the mayor! And then we saw his pajama pocket was stuffed with sweets, and his mouth was all gooey with sugar n' that. Ugh. So we said, 'Saving the robot from what, Percival?' And then he told us. *You!* All by yourself. You'd attacked it and all! We couldn't've believed it, really! But we did! And so we . . ."

"We punched him, we punched him," said Jackie Daw, pounding the cubicle curtain with his fists.

"And then we found this key," said Anna Daw, "around his neck, on a gold chain, so we asked him what it was but he wouldn't tell us—you should've heard him squeal! So we gave it a big yank, and the chain broke and Percival was hollering, and it was a really small key, and then we saw a padlock on the fridge and it was really small and it fitted the key, and we opened it up, and Percival was really blubbering by now, and he was bright pink, you should've seen him, and then we looked in the fridge and you've never seen anything like what was in there, I never *thought* of anything like it, you tell, Solly . . ."

"There was *ice cream!*" shouted Jackie.

"Yes, yes, yes," said Solly. "You never saw nothing like what was in that fridge. I couldn't've believed it, there was cream and cakes and jelly and doughnuts and marshmallows and sausage rolls and . . ."

"Ice cream!"

"And there were bottles and bottles of this fizzy stuff," said Anna. "So what we did was, we gave Grub and Jackie an ice cream each, all to themselves, well, they took them anyway, and then we pelted Percival, yes, we really let him have it, yes, we got the cream and the cakes and the sausage rolls and ice cream and all that, and we squashed them all over Percival, we shoved them down his pajamas, on the insides, and then we squelched jelly in his hair, and then we poured the fizzy stuff all over him, oh, you should of seen the mess, it was terrible. . . ."

"It was wonderful wonderful wonderful," sang Jackie, jumping up and down. And then sitting on the floor he began to cry and said, "But we should of eaten it all ourselves!"

"So now Percival's sleeping in a little cot in Mrs. Padlock's room," said Solly, "and I've seen him peering around the door. His hair's been washed and greased down on that ugly head, with this dinky doo-dah curl in front. Ugh. We got really punished by them down there, but it don't mean nothing."

"We got punished, yes," said Anna, "but it was worth it."

Johnnie pushed back the blankets and sat on the edge of the bed. He was covered with bruises that were turning dark gray and yellow.

"And Archibald?"

"Archibald is still the same . . . well . . . almost. . . ."

"Does he still hit everybody?"

"Oh, yes, as hard as ever."

"Then what I tried to do was useless," said Johnnie.

"You did your best."

"Then my best *wasn't good enough*!" shouted Johnnie, banging the blanket with his fist. "But I'm not giving up. Nobody knows about us, nobody cares about us, we've got to fight for ourselves!"

"But them down there is stronger!" said Solly. "And they've got all the weapons—we ain't got a thing!"

It was true. Johnnie turned his head away. The difficulties seemed to rise up before him like a brick wall. He felt as if he was a very small worm crawling along the base of the wall, and the Worthies were great birds sitting in a row along the top of the wall, looking down on him with scorn.

Mrs. Padlock's irritated voice could be heard calling up the stairs. Solly and the others ran off, leaving Johnnie alone.

He was parched. He took another sip of the dusty water left by Miss Stir and then, as a matter of habit, looked around for his geranium to water it, then remembered what had happened. He bent down and looked under the bed and found the pot with the broken stem. He was going to hide it away in a dark corner so as not to have to look at it again too soon, when he noticed, just around the base of the stem, two or three specks of bright, fresh green, the color of lettuce. Ah, so they hadn't destroyed everything. The geranium was still alive. He fed it a few drops of water and, getting up stiffly, set it in the window so that it could get some sun.

He looked out for a moment toward the forest, then turned back to the attic.

"I'll get up now," he said to himself, "and get on downstairs to help with the gadgets. We may as well put a few more spokes in a few more wheels while we're here."

73

11
ODD THINGS

"I always thought that Johnnie Rattle was clever with his hands," said Miss Stir to Shambles Methuselah one evening some days later. They were both picking nettles for soup, wearing motorcycling gloves to protect their hands from stings. "But now I notice that any machine he's been near seems more unreliable than it was before. I don't think that session with the robot did him any good at all."

Shambles grunted. Ever since it had trampled down his vegetable garden during the training session, he had hated the robot. He did not even like to hear it mentioned. He stuffed a great handful of nettles into a string bag.

"I don't think it did the robot much good either," went on Miss Stir. "There's something very slightly haywire in its mechanism. The Reverend noticed it himself. He rang up the Useful Machine Factory for advice, but he got a message that the number was disconnected. He wants me to overhaul the thing myself."

"The thing should be dismantled and put down the garbage disposal," said Shambles, thrashing the air with a great bunch of nettles. "Or turn it into a scarecrow. Great metal clodhopper that it is."

Some days later, the disinfectant episode occurred. It was late in the afternoon, and Johnnie and Solly were cleaning the gadget tubing in the hall, when suddenly Archibald appeared above them at the top of the stairs. In the crook of one arm was a box on which was written: DISINFECTANT SOAP. 2 DOZ. With his free hand he dipped into this box and extracted a bar of the soap, which he launched down the stairs, narrowly missing Solly's ear.

"Hey!" yelled Solly. "Wotcha doing with them things? *Hey!*"

Another bar hurtled down the stairs, then another. Soap was ricocheting off the walls and banisters, hitting the light and bouncing off the ceiling. Reverend Slipper came storming out of the front room. As if his appearance had cut an electrical connection, Archibald stood stock-still in mid-throw, one arm poised. The big fringed eye stared blankly ahead.

"How dare you stand there doing nothing, you idle orphans!" shouted the man. "What have you done to the robot? Get down on your knees and pick up that soap!"

75

Mrs. Padlock, who had been snoozing under a copy of *The Orphan Owners' Gazette,* now pottered out into the hall, expostulating and tutting. Johnnie and Solly picked up the soap and Reverend Slipper rather gingerly managed to inveigle the robot back into the laundry room. The boys were sent back to the attic, the soap was stored, and Reverend Slipper and Mrs. Padlock went back to the front room to recover from the ordeal. They had not been sitting down more than two minutes when there was the most stupendous crash from the hall. They rushed out. There, on the floor, in several pieces, lay the barometer. The glass was smashed to smithereens. This time they could not blame Archibald, and there was not a child in sight.

"Look at the mess! What shall we do to know the weather now?" cried Mrs. Padlock. "We shall have to get a new barometer from the catalog. We must keep track of the weather!"

Reverend Slipper stood looking down at the shards of glass. Eventually he said, "Would you be so kind as to fetch the dustpan, the brush, and a large bag, Mrs. Padlock, and remove the debris personally, by hand. Not so much as a splinter must remain."

He turned on his heel and strode into his study across the hall, slamming the door behind him. Mrs. Padlock started to sweep up the glass. Suddenly she froze, gazing into the gloom of the corridor which led to the kitchen. Her eyes were goggling. She put her hand to her head. What had happened? A great guffaw had suddenly seemed to come at her from all sides, booming into her skull. She blinked, and the noise stopped abruptly. "Migraine," said Mrs. Padlock to herself. "I certainly need that holiday."

At the same moment, out in the vegetable garden, where the late afternoon sun covered everything in a fuzzy golden haze, Shambles Methuselah was sitting in the pagoda having a quiet smoke to keep off the gnats, when he saw a figure by the kitchen door. For a moment he could not decipher the blur, but then he realized it was big Marvin, slouching in the doorway. The man looked as if he was going to slip down the doorpost and fall asleep on the step, but then he suddenly strolled off, through the vegetables, over the side hedge and away, in the direction of the forest.

"I think it was only a hiccup!"

"Thank you, Miss Stir," said the Reverend. "Due to your ministrations all seems to be working smoothly once more, though I could wish the robot a little less lax in administering discipline. Perhaps it is the heat. Let us hope the fine weather holds out until the Governors' Visit, which will soon be upon us."

A week had passed since Archibald had hurled the soap. Everything seemed to have calmed down. Percival had been sent back to the attic with a pair of binoculars and a baby alarm for protection.

One hot afternoon, at the end of the week, Mrs. Padlock programed Archibald to give a lecture on the Boons of Empire and then went downstairs for a lemonade and a chance to unlace her boots. Mrs. Padlock's lessons on Boons of Empire were invariably made up of scraps of history and readings from *Work in the Great Harvest Field,* interspersed with extracts from moldering letters which purported to come from reformed natives or bygone Missionary Orphans.

Archibald's lecture seemed to be proceeding along much the same lines: " . . . and in the town of Balyhoo Bala and in the hamlets surrounding Balyhoo Bala, and in the far-flung forest of Karmativi the streets are thronged with grateful natives singing 'Hey ho the stones of Empire shall never be unshook they teach us how to tie a tie and how to read a book the name of Carstairs and Bungho will always give rise to praise amen amen amen amen through all the summer days. . . .' "

That sounds remarkably like Mrs. Padlock's style, thought Johnnie.

" . . . for though darkness reigns through all the corners of the globe the little candle that is Carstairs and Bungho will never be obliterated for there nestling at the edge of the metropolis upright in its majesty and filled with love sits venerable Parchment House from whence many generations of happy orphans have come to relieve the darkness of a million natives and so we give thanks to those dedicated humbly to the welfare of others and we would like to say on this occasion that Reverend Slipper is a silly old kipper and a silly old kipper is he. . . ."

There was a whirring noise and Archibald stopped. Johnnie stared, frowning. *What* had he just heard?

After a kind of mechanical hiccup the robot went on. There was a lot more about waving palms and deep lagoons where once the unhappy native crouched in ignorance whereas now upright he can see the light of the sun with his own two eyes thanks to the selfless policy of Carstairs and Bungho " . . . and we will be ever mindful of the boon wrought by those pursuing fruitful paths and we will maintain forever that Mrs. Padlock is a smelly old *haddock*. . . . "

A grinding noise came from the vicinity of where Archibald's ears would have been if he had had any. Most of the orphans had not been attending at all and the word "haddock" startled them. Boons of Empire did not usually refer to haddock.

Archie went droning on, but right in the middle of a homily on the salvation of cannibals he started talking in a higher, more manic tone, rather like the gramophone when its handle had been turned too fast: "Half a pound of twopenny mice half a pound of treacle Padlock is a lobster's aunt pop goes the weasel Tweedle Dum and Tweedle Dee resolved to have a battle ugh they said this soup is bad it's made of rotten cattle just then came by a monstrous crow which ho ho oh no blow blow oh oh wheeeeeeeeeeeeeeeeeeee oh dear oh dear oh eeeeeyieeeeeeeeyiooooooooooooooooooooooooooooooh!"

Silence.

Was that smoke coming out of Archibald's plume? The children sat in silence and stared. A fly was crawling up the window. It crept from pane to pane on its tiny feet, then hung in the top corner, buzzing. An airplane, taking up the drone, flew miles and miles away in the blue sky, over and away from Parchment House, heading for the sea.

Mrs. Padlock came in.

"What! The lesson is over? That was quick! I hope you've got it all down. The Governors will be looking for good, neat work when they make their Annual Visit."

The children looked at Archibald, then looked at each other, sideways, without moving their heads. What was going on? The robot had a bland, efficient air. Butter wouldn't have melted in that metal mouth, but would have stayed nice and cool, as in a covered butter dish in a dark kitchen.

The time came to get Parchment House ready for the Governors' Visit. All the rooms had to be thoroughly cleaned, the garden weeded, the compost heap spruced up. The Reverend told Shambles Methuselah to get rid of his disreputable straw hat. The gardener aired his grievances to Miss Stir.

"And what keeps you here, Mr. Shambles?"

"It's a safe job, and things are hard nowadays. But I sometimes wonder. . . . I have never been more than twenty miles beyond Carstairs and Bungho in all my life . . . my whole life. . . . "

"I lived far from here at one time," said Miss Stir. "Farther south. My father was a military man. We traveled. Though my memory is somewhat hazy. I find that about Parchment House—one forgets, bit by bit, everything that did not happen here."

Shambles Methuselah thought of what it was like whistling along the road on his scooter in the evening when the sun was going down over Carstairs and Bungho. He thought of the cows champing in the fields under the shadow of the fuel reactors, and of the tourists in their Bermuda shorts flattening themselves into the hedgerow as he whirred past, and of the sea wind blowing grit into his eyes. Perhaps it would one day be possible just to keep traveling.

"Have you ever thought of leaving, Miss Stir? Do you still have family elsewhere?"

"I have no family left. I am an orphan, like these others, to tell the truth."

They sat together on the compost heap, while Shambles finished his tea.

"Would you like to take a spin on the back of my motor scooter some evening? You will need a helmet, of course."

Miss Stir gave a small sigh. All her life she had had a secret image of herself creating havoc by riding a gold-plated Harley-Davidson at a hundred miles an hour through sleepy villages from one end of the country to the other. Shambles's motor scooter was the next best thing.

"I shall make a special trip to town to buy one."

*   *   *

On the day before the Governors' Visit, when everybody should have been checking and polishing and getting Archibald ready to perform for the visitors, Miss Stir was nowhere to be found. She returned to Parchment House as the shadows were growing longer and more blurred. Instead of entering the house she walked around the back. In the rough track that edged the vegetable garden Shambles revved up his scooter. In her new red crash helmet, Miss Stir came down past the vegetables and pushed through a hole in the hedge. Shambles looked at her admiringly.

"You look game for anything, Miss Stir."

"Game for a ride on a scooter any day."

They bumped down the track and out through the gate to the high road. They whizzed beyond the boundaries of Carstairs and Bungho. Bats flicked past their heads. A fox in the grass fields along the road watched them pass. The moon came out, a full moon, its brilliance unlike the color of anything on earth.

All night, far and wide, the scooter's headlamp cut swaths along the lanes.

12
GOVERNORS' DAY

It was Governors' Day. The sky was cloudless.

Reverend Slipper rose briskly. He put on a fawn suit, a new collar, and a pair of shining black pointed shoes. He combed his hair down sleek over his big skull, and arranged a black handkerchief in the breast pocket of his suit. Then he went downstairs to inspect the house.

Everything glistened. The dining room in particular was a masterpiece. A slap of paint had brightened up the walls, and several mementos of Empire had been hung up to decorate them. In the middle of the big table was a pyramid of plaster fruit. How beautiful it all was! There were napkins folded into fan shapes, crystal wine glasses, finger bowls, toothpicks in narrow canisters. The big porcelain plates were decorated with a monogram saying "PH," and the motto "Ever Humble" set in a wreath of flowers held by two doves. Pink carnations and ferns were arranged in tall silver vases, and at each end of the table were laminated plastic cruets set on the backs of brass elephants. A fancy menu card was standing in the middle of the table, next to the plaster fruits. What grandeur!

Reverend Slipper finished inspecting the ground floor and went upstairs to check the schoolroom. As he climbed the stairs he thought over all that had been done: cupboard full of notebooks; rooms all polished; compost heap under a clean sheet; list of orphans ready for export to Balyhoo Bala—what else was there to remember? Surely nothing could go wrong. "I must quell my tendency to be a perfectionist," he told himself, leaning against the window frame in the schoolroom, idly watching the Bird Table, more as a matter of habit than out of a desire to catch anything at that particular time. The vegetable garden was already under a heat haze. The vegetables looked a bit limp, but the hedge was shiny, as if it was sweating slightly.

As the Reverend gazed at the sunlit scene a great shadow suddenly floated over the garden. There was no noise to accompany it, and no general darkening of the air as there is before a storm.

The shadow was rippling like a vast flag over the vegetable garden and vanishing over the hedge. The Reverend pried open the window and peered out at the sky. He could see nothing for the moment—that is to say, *nothing at all*. It was as if he was completely blind. Then his eyes cleared and above him was the flawless sky, with nothing passing over it but two tiny clouds, moving seaward over the house, in the direction opposite to the shadow. The Reverend peered into the distance, but beyond the hedge the unblemished countryside stretched away, gold and green in the sunshine.

He wondered if he ought to see an eye doctor. He banged the window down so hard it nearly bounced out of its frame, then shook his head from side to side until he felt dizzy, rubbed his eyes and peered all around the room. His heart was beating a little fast. Otherwise, everything appeared to be normal. The new collar chafed his throat where he had given himself a particularly close shave. He had a slight headache. He stroked his faintly oily forehead. It must be this confounded heat, he thought, wiping his face all over with a black handkerchief.

A sudden noise, coming from the laundry, broke the silence. He strode from the schoolroom and nearly crashed into Miss Stir, who was also on her way to the laundry room. He noted with distaste that, Governors' Day or no Governors' Day, she was still wearing her overalls, and not even clean ones at that. In fact she looked decidedly dusty. Anyone would think she had spent the night in a hedge.

They entered the laundry room together to find Archibald rocking to and fro, squeaking like a rocking horse. The robot was dressed to kill, with a carnation in the buttonhole of his new suit, and a bowtie with pink spots.

"Don't tell me he has been left on all night, Miss Stir! His power will be running low! His performance will be unpredictable!"

"Of course his power isn't too low," said Miss Stir

crossly. "Probably he's got too much power and is, so to speak, brimming over with it!"

She twiddled a mechanism in the robot's back. Archibald stopped rocking and only twittered slightly.

"Everything prepared, Miss Stir? Incidentally, I trust you will be quite happy to take your meal out in the pagoda with Mr. Shambles, after you have supervised the robot's speech, of course?"

"Herrumph," grunted Miss Stir.

"Is there anything wrong with the thing?"

"Absolutely not. He is in the most tiptop condition imaginable. You can count on Archibald."

The Reverend looked at Archibald. The robot stared back, its eye impassive, its clenched teeth gleaming.

There was nothing more to do. Reverend Slipper strolled downstairs and leaned against the newel post, waiting for the orphans to assemble in the hall for Orphan Inspection.

The orphans had been scrubbed with a green substance that burned their eyes and scalps, and their nails had been scraped down to the quick. Only Inky was impervious to the green stuff and remained the same bluish color he always was.

"Oh, you horrible, dirty creature!" said Mrs. Padlock, thumping him with the brush. "Ugh. Keep behind the others."

The Carstairs and Bungho Scouts Group had held a special rummage collection for local orphans. A great pile of sweaters darned at the elbow with odd wool, old shirts, blue jeans with the hems cut off, enormous flowered overalls, permanent press pants, and lacy bed jackets had been delivered to Parchment House. The orphans were given an outfit each, and then told to line up in the hall. Reverend Slipper inspected them.

"Very creditable, Mrs. Padlock. They look clean and pious. But what a miserable set of expressions. Let's have a bit of joy!"

"What I say about orphans, Reverend, is that they know not what side of the bread their jam is buttered on."

"I couldn't have put it better myself. Now, to start the day on a happy note, I shall address them with a few words on the Human Condition. Orphans, we have sailed the great ship of Parchment House through troubled waters, to be granted safe harbor on this happy day! Soon we will sally forth once more into uncharted seas in this great adventure called Life. Look, orphans, the door of Parchment House has been flung open so that you may gaze on Nature's Glories. I must emphasize, however, that if any one of you so much as sets a toe over the threshold before being ordered to do so, he or she will be torn to ribbons. Thank you, Mrs. Padlock, for everything. Aha, I hear the caterers approach. Stand back, children! Do not fidget!"

A truck drew up at the gate. Here came the Governors' Day lunch. Mouth-watering gusts of smell came up the path. The caterers' boys, smartly dressed in white overalls and tall hats, were bringing in the food.

The children looked on in astonishment. Their heads swiveled this way and that. Where on earth did all this food come from? There were plates of ham and salami and smoked salmon, and fishes in brown jelly, and little fluted pies. A prawn slice dripping with pink sauce was borne in, closely followed by a silver tureen piled high with yellow potatoes slathered with mayonnaise. There were pickles and beets and tomatoes carved like flowers, and hundreds of different kinds of potato chips in silver bowls, and big straw baskets of bread: long loaves and fat, round loaves and crescents with flaky, yellow-brown crusts and tiny buns covered with sesame seeds.

Then *something*—some great and wonderful masterpiece—was carried in, hidden under a silver dome, on an enormous silver platter. This dish was so unwieldy that it had to be supported by four caterers' boys—two at each end.

But it was the puddings that were beyond belief. There were jellies shaped like rabbits and castles, in the depths of which glimmered mysterious hunks of fruit; a chocolate mousse thickly covered with curls of grated chocolate; pink and white meringues on a green plate shaped like the leaf of a water lily; and custards wobbling in cut-glass bowls. But most beautiful of all, rising above the top of a golden dish, there trembled a clover-colored strawberry soufflé, its surface packed with fruit and icing sugar and whorls of cream.

Last of all came a very small caterers' boy carrying a massive wooden board covered with wedges of every sort of cheese, and a dish of butter, and piles of crisp crackers arranged around the edge.

The orphans looked on in silence as the food was brought in. They felt dizzy. Then Grub let out a howl such as a small dog might make when tied up and left all alone at midnight in a junkyard. The howl was soon squashed, however, by Mrs. Padlock taking a hairbrush out of her sweater pocket and belaboring him with it.

At last the caterers left. Reverend Slipper looked at the children's faces. He felt immensely satisfied. Smells of food drifted into the hall from the kitchen. Jackie Daw sniffed, and Anna wiped his face with the sleeve of the bed jacket she had been given to wear. It was very hot in the hall. The grass outside looked beautifully green.

"Stand up straight," said Reverend Slipper. "Let us proceed with our plans for the day. I have selected one boy—oh lucky boy—to share our lunch with us and partake of all the nice food, and to tell the Governors all about Parchment House. I feel we should have an orphan representative at the table. Percival Amalgam, step forward. It is you who have been chosen."

Percival Amalgam, who was wearing a new sailor suit ordered from Mrs. Padlock's catalog, sidled heavily forward.

The other orphans looked at him with envy and disgust.

"Sit by Mrs. Padlock and be a good boy, as you always are, Percival. You others," said the Reverend, glaring at them, "are to stand as you are, not moving, until the Governors arrive. After that you are to disport yourselves on the lawn and do some dances symbolizing happiness and contentment. Simultaneously with dancing, you will utter wondrous cries, for Governors' Day is celebrated thus among us, with green grass and open air for every happy orphan. If you do not behave yourselves you will be locked in irons for a week and fed on crumbs and water. Any money saved on your keep I shall send to the Fund for the Dissemination of Divine Knowledge in the Foothills of the Ganda Ganda Territories. Thank you. That is all."

The children stood motionless and silent, not daring to move a muscle, though Solly Turk could just be heard to mutter under his breath: "Percival Pig, Percival Pig . . ." Johnnie felt his face grow cold and shivery with rage, even though it was so warm. All that beautiful food, and not a scrap for the orphans. He clenched his hands so hard he could feel the scrubbed nails digging into his palms, and he ground his teeth together to keep himself from shouting out that it was unfair! Unfair! But all he could do was stand in the sunlit hall and wait. The Governors would soon be here.

13
THE FEATHER PANTRY

After sherry at the civic center the three Governors set out for Parchment House in the official limousine. In the trunk were thirteen straw baskets lined with blue silk and filled with exotic chocolates for the orphans. The handles of the baskets were decorated with bows, so that when it was open the trunk looked like a field of holly-blue butterflies.

The three Governors, Mr. Grymm, Mr. Pramme, and Lady Vanilla-Vyne, sat on the back seat. Lady Vanilla-Vyne, who had only just been elected Governor, was a large lady in a fur coat and a big straw hat decorated with a dead pigeon and some velvet cherries. Mr. Grymm and Mr. Pramme had been Governors for many years. Both of them were dressed in gray suits with mother-of-pearl buttons, gray bow ties, kid gloves, and suede shoes. Mr. Grymm was tall, with a cadaverous face, a blue chin, and eyes like a vulture, whereas Mr. Pramme was rather small and pink.

The countryside glittered darkly as the car drove along the dusty road toward Parchment House. The only other vehicle they passed was a rag-and-bone cart, whose occupant was unshaven, and apparently singing. Really, thought Lady Vanilla-Vyne, it was extraordinary that such examples of old world charm should still be permitted to roam around at large, especially as there was a Certified Garbage Disposal and Sanitation Department to deal with all that kind of thing. She fanned her hot face and gazed out through the dark glass.

Back at Parchment House, all had been ready for some time. Big Marvin had come down from his room wearing a black suit that had seen better days. He wore dark glasses and a pair of battered tennis shoes. He leaned against the radiator, picking his teeth with a fragment of match. Archibald had been led downstairs by Miss Stir, and they both stood to attention beside the pale mark left by the disappearance of the barometer. The children were faint with heat and nerves. Mrs. Padlock had grown very red. Reverend Slipper had a welcome grin fixed securely on his face.

The purring of a car could be heard coming nearer and nearer. It stopped. A door banged. The Governors had arrived!

Mr. Grymm came first, then Lady Vanilla-Vyne. At the back was Mr. Pramme, who was loaded up with all the chocolates—they dangled from his fingers and hung from his buttons and were piled up in his arms, so he was almost hidden behind them. The Governors were no sooner in the house—in fact Mr. Pramme was still on the doorstep—when Miss Stir pressed the robot's START button and Archibald gave a clattering sigh and launched into his speech:

"It is with great pleasure that we welcome you here O Governors of the Realms of Carstairs and Bungho Glory be to the Governors and all who sail in them we have here an orphan factory a wondrous institution designed to make silk purses out of sows' ears and worse rest assured that of all so generously poured into the coffers of Parchment House not a penny is wasted we are ever mindful of the welfare of orphans so cruelly deprived by fate and hazard and bad management of the kind strict overseeing eye usually found rooted in the family hearth with its mantelpiece with the clock on it to remind us of the passing of time it does not go on forever and photographs of family to remind us of the heritage of the ages and the need to honor our elders and betters the bunches of flowers in pots and vases to remind us of Nature's Bounty the other delights of the family hearth a fire in the grate magicoal or electric for example however to return to the subject of our peroration namely the relationship of the orphans with your gentle selves who work hard in order that these deprived morsels of humanity may grow in comfort and guidance and find a substitute hearth here beneath the portals of Parchment House here where we welcome you today with for your refreshment turkey curried with kiwi fruit garnish and wine and strawberries and . . ."

Reverend Slipper lifted his eyebrows at Miss Stir. After all, a perfectly adequate menu card had been provided.

". . . to entertain you tales of all the merry pranks the orphans get up to in their leisure hours spent polishing scrubbing starving ha ha you don't believe me? no no my little joke and how many miles to Babylon? What's the time, Mr. Fox? It's Dinner Time it's Dinner Time and if you listen hard you will hear under these hallowed portals the happy laughter of generation upon generation of happy childhood being prepared for the deserts of Balyhoo Bala and the mountains of Hideyhangoo little do they know what awaits them the happy orphans as they sing about their daily business and perform their little tasks not heeding the outside world and not heeded by it either eh what free of responsibility careless reckless the happy orphans whistle while they work and that is why you will hear rising it seems from the roof tiles and through the chimneys of Parchment House a kind of whistling and drone and constant joyful whine of heedless mirth listen listen can you hear it a wail a boohoo of quashed hopes of dusty food of devoured time of denied humanity of freedom's assassination ha ha my little joke listen listen can you hear it as the night stalks the field as the foxes sit in the stalks of oat grass, as the moon foxes the field as the little night moths . . . ?"

Reverend Slipper lunged for the STOP button.

"Thank you, thank you. An offering, ladies and gentlemen, in the inimitable style of Archibald, our humorous robot."

An anguished groan came from the doorway where Mr. Pramme, half-buried under baskets of chocolates, sweltered in the heat.

"Come in, come in, and thank you so much," said Reverend Slipper. "We will enjoy those in the evening when the children are abed."

"Oh, but these are *for* the children," said Lady

93

Vanilla-Vyne, beaming around at everyone. "They have been brought with money raised by the Round Table Club of Carstairs and Bungho as a kind gesture of support for the orphanage."

"Oh, how thoughtful. Take the chocolates into the kitchen, Mrs. Padlock, dear, and lock them in the fridge for later."

The Governors and Reverend Slipper shook hands, and Lady Vanilla-Vyne introduced herself, and then she went mincing heavily up and down rows of children, patting their cheeks in a vague manner. By the time she had got around all the children she seemed slightly put out.

"So these are the orphans? How sweet. But they do look a teeny bit . . . What do they look . . . ? How would you say they looked, Mr. Grymm?"

"As well-behaved and clean as last year. Empire material. Undoubtedly. Very fine."

"They look to me just the mimsiest wee bit . . . *thin*," said Lady Vanilla-Vyne. "Where are all the red cheeks and chubby limbs I expected to see? However, perhaps they are happy enough inside. Tell me, little ones, are you a happy band of orphans?"

There was silence.

"Come now, Percival, tell Lady Vanilla-Vyne all about . . ."

But Johnnie Rattle could bear it no longer. He darted up to Lady Vanilla-Vyne and, shoving his face under the brim of her hat, he cried, "You don't want to listen to Percival. Percival is a spy. Ask *us*, us here. *They* torment us; they make us live worse than insects. Flies get more to eat than us. We'd be much happier living in a ditch."

A murmur started to ripple through the orphans. Reverend Slipper snapped into action.

"Enough!"

He grabbed Johnnie and held him in a grip that made it impossible even to squeak. With a grin so oily that it seemed about to slide off his face, the Reverend turned to the Governors.

"Ah, well. One is bound to have one bad apple in a basket of blooming fruit. This child has always proved a problem. It only underlines our amazing feat in achieving a ninety-nine percent success rate in the production of exportable Missionary Orphans. This one would, I am afraid, disgrace a pigsty."

He covertly gave Johnnie's arm a twist which brought tears of pain to the boy's eyes.

"I am really looking forward to showing you all around our happy establishment. But before I manifest to you a few specimens of the orphans' work prior to luncheon, I must just go and give this little jackanapes a lecture on the subject of truth and manners. Excuse me. . . ."

As the Reverend dragged him away, Johnnie looked despairingly at the robot. Archibald stared back, dumb, dead, a steel box. But just as Johnnie was torn from the room, the robot, as once before, lowered the fringed lid over the great ball of its eye. The movement was so swift that no one else noticed. But the whole hall seemed suddenly changed to Johnnie, as if a great flood of light had poured through it, a light quite different from the sunlight that was shining on the garden outside.

It only lasted a second. The grip on his arm was implacable. As he dragged the boy down the corridor toward the kitchen, Reverend Slipper bent down and hissed into Johnnie's ear, "I shall lock you up for now. But after the Governors leave I shall deal with you as you deserve. Ruin our day, would you? We shall see about that!"

He dragged Johnnie into the kitchen and hauled him across the stone flags and pushed him into a little pantry, just off the kitchen, throwing the boy on to a pile of sacks in the corner. Then he bolted the door from the outside. Through the wire grille high up in the pantry wall, Johnnie saw the Reverend look down on him for a second. The man's eyes seemed to gleam red in the gloom. Then he was gone.

Johnnie looked around the pantry. It was slightly larger than one of the cubicles in the attic. It smelled faintly of rotten meat. The floor was crammed with sacks. Piled on shelves and hanging from rusty hooks were leather pouches and leather bags. The dirt floor was covered with feathers. The sacks were tied with thin rope. Johnnie undid one and immediately a cloud of feathers floated up into his face, making him sneeze. They caught in his hair and stuck to his cheeks, and even got into his mouth, so he had to spit them out in disgust. He undid another sack, and then another. They were all full of feathers: brown, black, white, speckled; breast feathers and wing feathers—the plumage of thousands of birds. Johnnie untied the thongs drawn around the necks of the pouches. Inside were little piles of bright feathers: blue, green, orange, yellow. One tiny purse was full of tiny scarlet feathers.

There were so many! Where had they come from? Johnnie shivered. He felt that if he himself had been a bird and not an orphan, Reverend Slipper would have been happy to pluck him, storing his plumage here, and the rest of him . . . where . . . ?

He threw himself at the door. He rattled the latch, kicked the wood, banged with his fists. It might as well have been made out of concrete. It was not going to budge. Light shone through the grille. Johnnie piled up some sacks so that he could climb them and look out.

There, beyond the rusty wire, was the kitchen, with the feast spread out ready to be taken to the dining room. Right in the middle of the kitchen table was the great platter with the silver domed lid, and round about were laid out the plates and bowls of beautiful food, all covered with a gauze sheet to keep off the flies. The Flydevora machine whirled from the ceiling, its sticky silver tubes windmilling slowly beneath the muslin nets.

Up above his head, Johnnie could hear the faint stomping of feet. That would be the Governors, being shown the Archie Facts in the notebooks. Soon they would tramp down to gorge themselves. It was monstrously unfair.

There was the sound of footsteps from outside. Someone came in through the kitchen door from the vegetable garden. Johnnie shrank back against the wall, so that he could see into the kitchen without being seen. It was Miss Stir. She was dragging a full black garbage bag, while in the other hand she had a picnic basket on top of which was precariously balanced a watering can.

Miss Stir approached the kitchen table. Her movements were somehow stealthy for such a clodhopper of a woman. For a moment she gazed at all the food. Then she folded back the gauze and lifted the lid off the great silver platter. She laid the lid aside and in an abrupt movement tipped up the platter and emptied its entire contents into the picnic basket. She held the platter under the Kleenukwik spout for a moment, put it back on the table, lifted a large object out of the plastic bag, and placed this on the dish instead. She took a syringe out of her pocket and gave the object a quick jab, looked at her watch and grunted, then poured a kind of custard from the watering can over the object, snitched a few bibs and bobs from the salad dishes and arranged them on top of the yellow sauce. She surveyed her handiwork for a moment, then put the domed lid back over the whole structure and replaced the gauze.

Then Miss Stir picked up the picnic basket, the empty garbage bag, the watering can, and a bottle of wine from the sideboard and, laden down, left by the way she had come in.

As she walked out the back door Johnnie called out, but his throat was dry, and only a croak came out. Miss Stir had gone. The Flydevora whirled. A couple of flies, let in by Miss Stir, buzzed hopefully above the puddings for a moment, then the Devora sucked them in.

Johnnie heard another set of steps, approaching this time from the direction of the corridor. Big Marvin came into the kitchen. He had on a black hat, and carried a knapsack on his back. In his left hand was a very long canvas case. He looked vaguely as if he was going on a fishing expedition. For a moment he stood and gazed around the kitchen, then gave a kind of guffaw, picked a strawberry off the top of the soufflé, and went out through the back door, closing it gently behind him.

The apparition of big Marvin had been so swift and light-footed, it was as if a shadow had passed quickly through the kitchen.

The sacks started to slip under Johnnie's feet. To keep his balance he clutched at the rusty grille. A strand of wire seemed to crumble under his fingers, powdering them with ginger dust. He tugged at the wire, and a coil of it came away from the rotten wooden frame, loosening the pattern of the screen in one corner. Johnnie pulled harder, and another strand started to loosen. The whole grille was beginning to sag.

Slowly, fiercely, scratching and pricking his hands on the wire, Johnnie started to pull a hole in the grille.

14

A SEAGULL

The orphans had been sent outside to demonstrate glee on the front lawn, but they just hopped about like injured birds.

Reverend Slipper, seeing them from the landing window as he took the Governors upstairs, was disgusted. He would have liked to beat some *joie de vivre* into the creatures. Luckily, Lady Vanilla-Vyne was puffing so hard that she did not notice, and Mr. Grymm was busy writing things down in a notebook. Mr. Pramme never noticed anything anyway.

Reverend Slipper showed the Governors around selected spots, then took them to the schoolroom to inspect the books. He opened the cupboard swiftly to reveal the piles and piles of Archie Facts, then pulled out a couple of notebooks for the Governors to look over.

"What industrious children!" cried Lady Vanilla-Vyne.

"Ah, but it is the robot, Lady Vanilla-Vyne, who has lifted the work rate so substantially. Where would we be without him? Far, far less advanced in our quest to produce the perfect example of Missionary Orphanhood. He is a Renaissance man among robots!"

Seeing Mr. Grymm looking rather closely at a page of Archie Facts, Reverend Slipper flipped the book shut and gently extracted it from Mr. Grymm's grasp.

"I hope you find our progress satisfactory. But now perhaps you would like to share a meal with us. A taste of our home cooking, though of course a little more elaborate than is our normal fare, in honor of our guests."

"Lovely," said Lady Vanilla-Vyne, fanning herself with a pink-gloved hand.

They trooped downstairs. How bright and cheerful Parchment House looked in the sunshine! How clean it smelled!

It gave Reverend Slipper a nice feeling to think of Johnnie Rattle huddled in the darkness of the pantry, far far away from the sun.

They entered the dining room. Even Mr. Grymm looked slightly impressed with the display. Reverend Slipper was pleased to note that Miss Stir and big Marvin had tactfully absented themselves. He got everyone seated, then gestured grandly to Mrs. Padlock.

"Bring in the food! Now, Percival, you have an opportunity to tell Lady Vanilla-Vyne and Mr. Grymm and

Mr. Pramme all about our happy community here at Parchment House."

Percival made an effort to oblige. But his mind kept wandering off, and he started telling Lady Vanilla-Vyne a tale about how he wasn't really an orphan but the son of a king and queen who were traveling abroad at the moment but who would soon come and carry him off to a castle where he would live with lots of servants and they would have a long drive with a gatehouse so that people would have to call for permission before they were allowed to set foot inside the grounds and there would be guard dogs with big teeth that . . .

Even this species of drivel couldn't wipe the smile off Reverend Slipper's face. He managed to stop Percival by kicking him in the shin. The atmosphere was saved by the appearance of Mrs. Padlock bringing in dish after dish of beautiful food, finishing with the concoction on the silver platter.

With a flourish, Reverend Slipper hoisted the silver dome.

"Behold! Cold turkey in curry sauce!"

They all stared.

"That's a large type of fowl," said Mr. Grymm.

"Free-range, Mr. Grymm. Free-range, like our little orphans here."

Mr. Pramme cleared his throat nervously: "I say . . . It looks a bit . . . It can't still have . . . No, I must be wrong? . . . It can't be *feathers!*"

"Decorative flair from the chefs," said Reverend Slipper, wondering what the man was talking about. He peered at the glistening yellow heap in the middle of the platter. Well, maybe it did look a little odd, but after all, it was supposed to be a special dish—not chicken and chips, for goodness' sake.

He leaned across and pronged the fork deep into

the yellow mound, raising the carving knife to cut the first slice.

"Oh, Mrs. Padlock, the kitchen has done us proud in this . . ."

The rest of his sentence was completely wiped out as the mound gave a mewling cry and rose into the air, scattering fruit and capers and yellow sauce all over the place. The curried turkey was flying around and around the room. It blundered into the curtains, the newly painted walls, the ceiling, the rustic prints. There were yellow blobs everywhere. The pyramid of plaster fruits got smashed and the flower vases got knocked over, so that water and ferns and carnations went every which way. Eventually the bird perched on top of the curtain rod and looked down at them, scrunched up and miserable, its beady eyes just visible beneath the curry sauce that was dripping from its head.

"That's not a turkey at all!" cried Mr. Pramme.

"No, I'd say not," said Mr. Grymm, taking his notebook from his pocket and scribbling a few words.

Lady Vanilla-Vyne's face had gone completely blank. She was holding tight with both hands to her hat.

"I'd say," said Mr. Pramme, ". . . well, I don't know. . . . Do you have a *Book of British Birds* handy? Well, really . . . What would you say it was, Bernard?"

"A seagull," said Mr. Grymm.

"Oh, do open the window, quick quick quick, and let the poor thing out!" wailed Lady Vanilla-Vyne, staring at the bird in terror.

Mrs. Padlock managed to get the window open. The bird thumped once more around the room and then flew straight out, leaving a piece of kiwi fruit on the ledge.

There was a stunned silence. Then Mr. Pramme coughed nervously. It was not every day one saw one's

102

dinner flying out of the window under its own steam.

For a moment Reverend Slipper just sat there, the knife and fork held in the air in front of him, staring at the empty dish. He was completely unable to think of anything to say. It was as if his brain had flown out of the window too. He turned and gazed out over the sunlit vegetable garden, as if to call it back. There were Miss Stir and Shambles, sitting on the pagoda steps, eating something. They appeared to be laughing. It was all very well for some. However, one must carry on. He shook his head to get rid of the feeling, then smiled at everyone.

"A joke! A joke! Some merry prankster has been putting one over on us! Now let's get going on the *real* food!"

But the salads and the prawn slice and the little fishes in brown jelly and all the other delicacies had somehow lost their luster. Everyone looked a bit suspiciously at the food on their plates, as if it might come to life too.

In the base of the Reverend's skull an ominous throbbing had started, a tom-tom of rage. Somewhere along the line he had been made a fool of. Someone would have to pay. He looked closer at his plate. In the depths of a piece of lettuce, curled up as if it was asleep, lay a very small and hairy caterpillar.

What was going on? A source of corruption was at work in the depths of Parchment House. It must be rooted out and destroyed forever! He picked up a teaspoon and hit the already defunct caterpillar until it was flattened.

He grinned and grinned, and tried to make polite conversation, but rage was in his heart.

103

15
HAVOC!

Johnnie twisted and tugged at the wire, pulling it loose from the frame and uncoiling strands where they were wound around each other, only stopping and shrinking into the shadows when Mrs. Padlock came in to collect the first course and take it in to the Governors. The silver platter was so heavy she tottered under its weight.

When she had gone, Johnnie went on pulling frantically at the wire with his sore fingers. At last the hole was big enough. He hauled himself up, wriggled through the grille, and fell head first into the kitchen.

He looked at the sunlit vegetable garden through the kitchen window. For once, the back door was un-locked. He could escape. By keeping near to the wall he could get around the front and away across the lawn and down the road before anyone spotted him. But something stopped him—it was no good running away. It was no good just getting up and leaving, abandoning the others to the fate of being bullied for years and then turned into Missionary Orphans. Besides, he wanted to get back at Reverend Slipper.

But what could be done?

He looked at the puddings, glimmering under the gauze. The slippery sides of the jellies gleamed as if they were alive. He stepped toward the puddings, folded back the gauze, and stretched out his hand, the little finger curled to scoop a morsel, just a morsel, of jelly, of chocolate, of cream. He just wanted to know what they were like. But a strange thing happened. He could not touch them. He could not eat. The puddings were like something on the other side of a pane of glass. For years and years food had been nettle soup and stale crusts and maggoty pie. Now that real, glistening, lus-cious food lay within his reach, Johnnie could only look at it. He felt like crying.

Then he felt like smashing the puddings to bits!

But they were *too beautiful.*

A buzz of voices came through the wall. Ah, so they were all enjoying themselves, were they?

"You can laugh," said Johnnie under his breath, "until you're blue in the face, but *you're not going to get the puddings.*"

And yet—how could it be stopped?

A faint shuffling clank came from the direction of the hall. Johnnie peered around the door and looked along the shadowy corridor. There, blocking the sun-

105

light that streamed in through the front door, stood Archibald.

"Archibald, come here," called Johnnie in a low voice.

To his surprise, the robot revolved on its axis and swayed down the corridor toward him. It clomped into the kitchen and stood there, grinning madly as usual. Just as an experiment, Johnnie whispered into the robot's microphone, "Hello, hello, hello, is there anybody there?"

A definite tremor ran through the robot, making its plume tremble. The hum of its motor went up a tone or two. Johnnie had a feeling of power.

There was the sound of clattering plates from the dining room. He would have to hurry. Johnnie quickly took a napkin and a large white apron from a shelf in the corner. He hung the napkin over the robot's arm and tied the apron around its waist. Then he picked up the bowl of chocolate mousse and placed it carefully between the robot's big hands. The metal fingers immediately closed around the bowl.

"Brilliant, Archibald. Now listen. When they open the door and start bringing out the plates from the first course, you are to go in there and serve them the pudding *yourself*. What I want you to do, Archibald, is to cause havoc. *H.a.v.o.c.* I want you to spoil their lunch. I want you to *really* mess it up. Have you got the message? *HAVOC*! And make sure of one thing: *They don't get to eat the puddings!*"

Johnnie heard the dining room door open and Mrs. Padlock's feet tapping toward the kitchen. He hid behind the door as she came in. She seemed surprised to see the robot all dressed up and ready to serve. In the condescending tone she usually used when she had to talk to Archibald she said, "I had not realized you were

106

part of the lunch agenda, Robot. Now behave nicely. I presume you are programed correctly. Carry the puddings in a neat manner—no spilling! Follow me."

Oh, help, thought Johnnie. Supposing her instructions override the ones I gave him!

The robot clanked after Mrs. Padlock, gripping the chocolate mousse in a very professional manner. Johnnie crept after them and hid in the shadows outside the dining room door. He could just see through the crack. To and fro the robot went between the kitchen and the dining room, carrying all the beautiful puddings. Its mad grin never altered. Its feet followed the same path: shuffle shuffle shuffle, clank clank clank.

"*Havoc!*" whispered Johnnie desperately as the robot went by with the strawberry soufflé. "Get it into your head—*havoc!*"

The robot made no sign of having heard. Mrs. Padlock shut the dining room door, but Johnnie managed to push it slightly open again. He peered through the crack. There they all were, alternately gazing at the food with greedy eyes and staring admiringly at the robot.

All the puddings were on the table. Archibald began to serve.

Archibald's appearance with the chocolate mousse had created an overwhelmingly good impression. The memory of the seagull was almost wiped out. Mesmerizing! Even Mr. Grymm looked interested. Reverend Slipper looked a little puzzled when the robot first entered, but then decided to bask in the admiration excited by Archibald. Well done, Mrs. Padlock! he thought.

As pudding after pudding was brought in, the Reverend relaxed somewhat. After all, he couldn't be blamed personally for what had happened to the curried turkey; it was obviously some kind of a joke, though if he found out who was responsible he would personally strangle him.

After a few sticky moments, the Governors' visit seemed to be coming to a glorious conclusion.

"You see," he said, gesturing proudly at the robot, "the infinite variety of the thing. Not only can it cover the whole spectrum of human knowledge, but when so desired it performs delicate, if menial, tasks with aplomb."

The Governors nodded. Lady Vanilla-Vyne even made a patting movement toward the robot as it went past, though she didn't dare to actually touch it.

"Jolly good," she said.

After carrying in all the puddings, Archibald went to the sideboard and brought out the gold-engraved pudding bowls. He handed them out, flicking the napkin over each one to remove any suspicion of dust. The Governors had never seen anything like it. They were already writing imaginary reports to the Authorities, praising the brilliance of this astonishing machine.

Johnnie Rattle, crouching outside the door, was getting frantic.

Archibald began to serve the meringues. He lifted each one off the serving dish without denting an iota of its stiff, delicate cushion. Then he began to serve out the jellies, the custards, the chocolate mousse. The Governors nodded approvingly. What precision in those great metal hands. How wonderful the modern world was! And the robot was so stunning to look at, with its great body in the smart suit, and the small apron, and the plume.

Outside the door, Johnnie bit his knuckles with frustration. Not only was the robot not messing things up, it was proving to be a massive hit.

"*Havoc!*" he whispered through the crack of the door, though he knew there was no way the robot could hear him.

If anything, Archibald appeared to be getting quicker and neater as he went around—the whole performance was like a production line. It was almost dementedly efficient, in fact. . . .

"Now, Archibald," said the Reverend a little edgily, "I think we've got enough for the meantime. There is no need to continue serving. We can always come back for seconds."

But Archibald did not appear to want to stop.

Reverend Slipper smiled at the Governors. He felt rather stupid talking to a robot.

"Come now, Archibald. Do you think you could demonstrate your skills at a slightly more easygoing pace? We are not in a hurry to catch a bus, after all!"

"Haste makes waste," said Mrs. Padlock usefully. "Recall the tortoise and the hare. It isn't always . . ."

The words faded on her lips.

The robot was careening dangerously. Little objects were starting to tinkle and crash to the floor, and everyone was getting so much in their bowls that the meringues at the bottom were completely flattened. The jellies and custards and mousse were all swirling together and beginning to spill over the edge.

Archibald hadn't started on the cheese and crackers yet. And he had not even touched the great pink strawberry soufflé.

"Enough! Enough!" shouted Reverend Slipper.

"Go on! Go on!" whispered Johnnie from behind the door.

Reverend Slipper lunged at Archibald and just managed to brush the STOP button in the robot's back.

The touch of his finger seemed to madden it. It was

not going to stop now until it ran out of steam completely. Everybody was growing dizzy looking at it, and Percival Amalgam was whimpering hysterically and holding his belly and saying he felt sick. Archibald grabbed the cheese and crackers in fistfuls, and started crumbling them all over the piled-up puddings in the bowls in a fairly random manner, as if he was scattering seed. There were pyramids of food getting higher and higher in the middle of everyone's bowl, and dribbles of custard were spreading out over the tablecloth, and there were clots of jelly and flecks of custard everywhere.

"Oh, dear, oh, dear, the pudding looked very nice. I don't need cheese and crackers at the same time!" said Mr. Pramme, trying to snatch his food.

"Stop, stop, stop!"

Reverend Slipper, his face blank with rage, rose from his chair and, picking up a nearby fork, hurled it at Archibald. The prongs hit the robot in the eye, rebounded off and spiked into Lady Vanilla-Vyne's fat hand before twanging to the floor.

aaaaa aaaaa

aaaaa   aaaaa

"AAAAAAaaaaa   aaaaEEEEEEK!"

wailed Lady Vanilla-Vyne. "We have come to a madhouse!"

At the blow from the fork, the robot's mechanism gave a screeching whine, like a cat with its tail caught in the door, and the whole thing shuddered as if an explosive charge had been let off inside it. It upturned Mrs. Padlock's chair so that she tumbled to the floor, then it punched Mr. Grymm, and pushed Mr. Pramme's head down until his nose was squashed into his pudding. Then, picking up the still untouched strawberry soufflé, it hurled the whole mass at Lady Vanilla-Vyne, so that that lady's face disappeared behind a curtain of pink froth, and a wad of strawberries and mush flew up and landed on top of her hat, next to the bird.

Then, before Reverend Slipper or anyone else could stop it, the robot lifted up the edge of the table and, whirring triumphantly, upended the whole caboodle over the wall-to-wall lilac carpeting.

It had to be admitted: Governors' Day Lunch was at an end.

16

THE GOVERNORS GO HOME

The dining room was strewn with mangled puddings, broken crockery, crackers, fragments of plaster fruit, wine and carnations, various people and some shattered finger bowls. The robot lay on its back, smoking gently. Reverend Slipper was the only person still sitting in his chair. He found himself gazing blankly at a watercolor of a cow under a tree. He was suddenly aware of stifled laughter from outside the door, and then a voice chanting softly: "Well done, Archibald, you did it, you did it, you did it!"

In a second he was across the room like a police dog, to grab Johnnie Rattle. The boy was crouched in the corridor, laughing and pounding his head with delight.

As he became aware of the Reverend coming toward him, Johnnie stopped crowing and tried to run, but his feet seemed to be riveted to the floor. He suddenly felt weak all over.

"So so so!" cried Reverend Slipper, grabbing the boy by the hair. "A regular little Houdini! Thought you'd mess around with dangerous forces that don't concern you, did you? Ah, but you will learn your lesson now, once and for all!"

Still holding the boy by the hair, the man called back into the room.

"Mrs. Padlock, dear, could you arrange for everyone to go to the front room and then we can all have some coffee. Thank you."

Then the Reverend hauled Johnnie into the kitchen and, uncoiling several lengths of rope from a cupboard, tied him up like a boned joint of meat.

"How lucky I remember knot work from my young days with the Moral Brigade!"

Reverend Slipper dragged Johnnie all the way up to the attic, upside down, so that the boy's head banged on every step. He pulled him right along the attic to his own cubicle. Then Reverend Slipper took the black handkerchief out of his breast pocket and tied it around Johnnie's eyes, for he was tired, very tired, of the expression that he saw there. Johnnie tried to bite the Reverend, he yelled at him, but it made no difference at all. When he had finished tying the handkerchief and checking the knots, Reverend Slipper shoved the boy under the bed with his foot. At last the job was done.

The first part, anyway. The child would never get out of that particular corner. He would have to lie there, in the dust, to await his fate.

Reverend Slipper was out of breath. He sat down on the bed. He looked around the dingy space. His eyes lighted on the red geranium. There was one flower just coming out. In normal circumstances he would have screwed the plant into a damp fragment, but now he just stared dreamily at it. How strange, he had never really been up here in the attic for more than a few minutes at a time. He got up and looked out of the little round window. Why, a completely new view! There was a small forest on the horizon. How odd, never to have seen this view before. This was not such a bad spot, away from the hurly-burly. Of course, the other orphans were generally up here, disturbing the atmosphere. Really it would have been better for them to be kept in an out-house, or a garage. It occurred to the Reverend that this would be a good place for a study. One could put a desk in place of the bed. The little window could be boarded up. Maybe, thought Reverend Slipper, I could do some creative work. Write a book about a life tending to the moral welfare of orphans. Maybe such a system could be extended throughout the land bringing fame and fortune in its wake. The problems of vandalism, the perils of so-called liberal thought, could be wiped out in one fell swoop, and the name of Reverend Slipper would go down in the history books.

His thoughts went back to the events of the day, and his head started to throb dangerously. Those confounded Governors were still downstairs, expecting polite conversation, no doubt. He would have to deal with Johnnie Rattle later. He wiped his forehead with his hand, since the handkerchief was otherwise engaged, got up and walked softly downstairs, smoothing the oily strands of his hair over his big scalp and breathing heavily. He marched boldly into the front room.

"Well, well, I am mortified to have allowed a machine into the house that has obviously not undergone the proper tests. I'd call the Sanitation Department this very minute and ask them to take it away immediately, but I suppose we must keep the bodywork if we are to ask for a refund. After all, the thing was purchased with the Authorities' funds. I really am most dreadfully sorry. Are you fully recovered, Lady Vanilla-Vyne? Such an unfortunate episode to have occurred on your first visit. This is no way for a normally glorious Governors' Day to have turned out."

"No, Reverend, it is not," interrupted Mr. Grymm. "A bad influence on the children. Food thrown about in such a wanton manner. Think of the starving millions. They would be glad of it. Very."

Lady Vanilla-Vyne was rubbing at the strawberry stains on her hat with a pink handkerchief. Every now and then her big body shook with the tremor of a sob.

Reverend Slipper decided to bring the visit to a speedy conclusion, and then to deal with the sources of the confusion. He would get Miss Stir to take the innards out of the robot, and then perhaps the shell of the machine could be useful, as a hat stand, possibly.

"Lady and gentlemen, I would have liked to show you around the vegetable garden, but time is catching up with us. Let us, as a parting gift, offer you the sight of the children frolicking on the lawn."

A couch had been drawn up to the window so that the Governors could watch the children playing outside. The Governors sat there sipping their coffee. There wasn't much to look at. The children were staggering about in a dreary manner. Reverend Slipper stormed outside.

"I have had enough! You look like a lot of demented sheep! *Sing! Dance! Be joyous!*"

The children drew closer together and stared sullenly at the Reverend, then Solly Turk stepped forward.

"We ain't joyous, we's just hot and hungry."

Reverend Slipper swiveled on his heel and marched back into the house and took out of the fridge a box of ice pops. These had been made by Shambles using diluted orange juice. Miniature flowerpots had served as molds, with bandages covering the holes in the bottom. For sticks Shambles had used the thin green stakes which serve to support tall plants. The dye from these had run into the ice-pop mixture and made curious stains, as if the orange was growing mold. Reverend Slipper marched back outside and threw the soggy box on the lawn.

"You don't deserve a treat, *far from it,* but since these were especially made for you to celebrate this day, you may have them now."

Grub crawled forward and picked up an ice pop. He sniffed it and then threw it on the lawn.

"Gimme a chocolate," he said.

Solly picked up the ice pop and threw it at Reverend Slipper.

"We don't want this rubbish. We want *food*! Give us them chocolates!"

"Chocolates? What chocolates?"

"Them chocolates what the lady in the big hat brought."

"Lady Vanilla-Vyne to you. Lady Vanilla-Vyne is a new Governor and does not yet understand our habits of thrift and self-control, so she made the understandable mistake of introducing some chocolates into the establishment. Don't worry, we shall dispense with them ourselves."

"No no no, no you don't, you don't dispense with nothing. Them's our chocolates. You know that. *We* know that. We want them chocolates, give us them now!" shouted Solly, stamping on the grass. The other orphans nodded their heads and muttered agreement.

Reverend Slipper was absolutely astounded to be talked to in this way. He glanced nervously at the window.

"You can have the chocolates when our visitors have gone," he snarled. "Now *dance,* or not only will you not have chocolates, you will have nothing but crumbs and water for a full two weeks and I shall . . ."

He was about to say: "I shall set the robot on you," when he remembered.

"Who cares? *I* don't!" shouted Solly. "And we don't get nothing but crumbs and water half the time anyway, so what's that. And we won't dance unless you give us your word on the chocolates. And we want Johnnie Rattle back, *now,* without your hurting him or *nothing.* And if you don't say yes we'll just lie down on the lawn and pretend we're dead, because we might as well be dead as live here like this with you and her in there, and that's what we all think, so there!"

The smaller children were so alarmed at Solly Turk talking like this that they hid behind Philadelphia, tugging at her skirt. But Philadelphia, her thin face drained of color, brandished her fist at the Reverend and said, "We want Johnnie Rattle back, and we want our chocolates!"

"Yes, we do," said Jane Pegg in a small voice. And then all the children started murmuring angrily, and

117

Tiggy actually snarled and snapped at the Reverend and clawed at the air as if she would like to scratch him to pieces.

"Very well. My word on the chocolates," he said hurriedly. "And if I say something, I mean it. Now start dancing and playing happily. As for Johnnie Rattle, forget about him for the moment. You can have him back later *if you behave yourselves.*

"Or some of him!" he muttered under his breath as he strode back to the house. Chocolates indeed! He'd show them!

He went back and stood at the window, watching the children. The Governors made no comment about the dancing. He could understand why. It was not an inspiring sight. Still, the afternoon was nearly over. Soon he could get everyone out of the house. This had been a bad bad day.

At last the Governors decided to leave. Nobody seemed to know quite what to say. Lady Vanilla-Vyne's face was streaky with dried tears, and she had traces of pink foam on her pearls. Mr. Grymm was still ominously writing things down in his notebook. Mr. Pramme looked frankly ill.

"Good-bye, good-bye, good-bye!"

The limousine drove off. Mr. Pramme attempted a half-hearted wave through the dark glass, but the others did not wave at all.

17
LOCKING UP

"**A** few little hitches, but I think it all ended happily," said Mrs. Padlock, gazing at the ruined dining room. Behind her, Percival was heaving with great snotty sobs.

"What are you talking about, woman? It was a disaster! This room looks like the Fall of Carthage! I suspect that come Monday morning we shall all be joining the line outside the unemployment offices in Carstairs and Bungho. We shall all starve!"

Percival let out a bawl.

"*Stop that dreadful noise!* Take the robot away! Out

of the house! Get it dismantled! Throw it over the hedge! Get out yourselves! Now. Out. *Go!*"

"Well, I never . . . oh, dear, oh, dear, dear me . . . Percival, come on then, you get the legs and I'll . . . oh, dear, oh, dear . . ."

Somewhere along the line the robot appeared to have divested itself of its clothes. It seemed quite without power. Mrs. Padlock and Percival pulled and shoved it through the kitchen and out the back. They tried to prop it up against the side of the house, but it just collapsed. Eventually they abandoned it in the beet bed. Mrs. Padlock was at a loss what to do next. Suddenly she became aware that the vegetable garden was full of children. They were looking at her rather strangely.

"What are you doing, lounging about out here? Your clean clothes will get covered with dirt. Get up and assemble in orderly rows. We shall soon be going back indoors to help clear up the mess."

But Solly stepped forward, his eyes shining.

"No!" he shouted.

Mrs. Padlock was amazed. Percival put his hands over his ears, shut his eyes, and started to blubber.

"Look how upset Percival is," said Mrs. Padlock. "You should be ashamed to frighten one of your little friends in this manner."

"He ain't my friend, and he ain't little. These is my friends. Here we all are, Mrs. P., and there's more of us than there is of you, and we've had enough. We don't want no more of it. And where's Johnnie Rattle, what have you done with him, you tell us that?"

There were mutterings of "No!" "That's right!" "You tell her, Solly!" "We've had enough!" "Too much, too much!" Even Jane Pegg had picked up a twig and was shaking it at Mrs. Padlock. Jane Pegg! Whatever was the world coming to? Mrs. Padlock was flummoxed.

"We're on strike from now on," said Solly Turk. "What we want now is our chocolates. And more than that, we want Johnnie Rattle. Now. We don't want nothing to happen to him, nothing at all."

"That's right!" "Give us back Johnnie Rattle!" "Gimme a chocolate!" "We're on strike!" "Give us Johnnie Rattle, Johnnie Rattle, Johnnie Rattle!" chanted the orphans.

Mrs. Padlock looked around for help.

"Miss Stir? Mr. Shambles? Archibald?"

Solly looked scornfully at the metal body in the beet bed.

"The robot's a goner, by the look of it. And Miss Stir and Shambles went off on the scooter some time back and it was loaded with luggage. They's gone, and it doesn't look like they'll be back, and so that's that, Mrs. Padlock. Now where's Johnnie Rattle, let's be having him!"

"You are a little terrorist!" shouted Mrs. Padlock. "You deserve to be annihilated in sulphur!"

"And you deserve to be dropped in a pigpen!" shouted back Solly Turk.

The other orphans laughed.

Mrs. Padlock had never been talked to in such a disgraceful manner. And as for laughter, it was unheard of! She was about to lecture Solly on gratitude and humility, when it occurred to her that there were rather a lot of orphans all together in one place, all staring at her with a kind of wild light in their eyes. They also appeared to have moved in closer.

"If I persuaded the Reverend to give you the chocolates," she said in a sweeter tone, "would you all agree to behave in a proper manner?"

Grub shouted, "I wanna chocolate ..." but Philadelphia picked him up and shook him gently.

"No, no, Grub, later. Just wait. You'll get your chocolates. We'll *take* the chocolates. They're ours. Only just wait."

"That's right, that's right," said Solly excitedly. "We'll take the chocolates ourselves. We'll take a crowbar to the fridge! But what we want now is Johnnie Rattle. We want him here, now, back with us. What you waiting for, Mrs. Padlock?"

Mrs. Padlock looked at the house. If she could only consult with the Reverend . . .

"Perhaps I could go and persuade Reverend Slipper to let the horrible little . . . to let Johnnie Rattle go, provided that . . ."

Bang! Clatter! Clang!

The window shutters on the ground floor of Parchment House suddenly slammed shut.

Mrs. Padlock shook off Percival and ran to the kitchen door and shook it ferociously. Then she scurried around the side of the house and hammered on the front door and rattled the handle and shrieked. She beat against all the shutters in turn until the sides of her hands were scarlet. But there was no response at all. At last she tottered slowly back down the vegetable garden. Glaring at the orphans, she summoned Percival to her side.

"Come, Percival. We shall shelter in the pagoda, away from this riffraff. Reverend Slipper will not let us stay out all night. He is probably having a nap."

The pagoda had a deserted air. On the step were two plates with yellow smears on them, two bowls stuck with meringue fragments, and two upturned wineglasses in which flies were crawling. Mrs. Padlock sat on a pile of magazines, and Percival huddled beside her.

The orphans ignored them, but sat on in the vegetable garden, watching the barred and shuttered house, watching and waiting, though what they were waiting for, no one knew.

For a long time, nothing happened at all.

After Mrs. Padlock and Percival had dragged the robot from the house, Reverend Slipper had locked the kitchen door after them and thrown the key down the garbage disposal. His head felt peculiar. It was as if he had a red rubber band around the outside of his skull, at just about the level of the top of his ears, a band that was being twisted tighter and tighter.

How quiet it was. The kitchen tap was dripping, and there was a faint buzz of insects, but no other sound. How nice it was to have the house to oneself, with no orphans or Governors cluttering up the place. He went into the front room and gazed for a while at the deserted lawn, littered with ice-pop sticks and dotted with orange stains. He pulled the curtains across the window.

He prowled through the rooms to make sure nobody had crept back inside. Parchment House was empty. Good.

He thought of Johnnie Rattle tied up under the bed. The child was a serpent in Paradise, a nasty germ in a nice healthy body—when such an apology for an orphan was dealt with, weeping and tribulation could cease. Parchment House could start working again toward its ultimate goal. In his mind's eye Reverend Slipper had a vision of an endless cavalcade of Missionary Orphans streaming into the sunset. It was time to close up the house. It was time to deal with the germ, the serpent.

Reverend Slipper slammed shut the front door and locked it firmly, then put up the long steel bars that acted as a double barrier and locked them into their sockets. Then he pushed the secret switches behind the curtains that activated the shutters on the outside of the downstairs windows. They clanged shut. Now everything was in darkness. The noise Mrs. Padlock made outside trying to get in seemed to come from far, far away. He scarcely noticed when it stopped. He stalked through the ground floor, checking for chinks and exits. He was perspiring slightly, as it was becoming a swelteringly hot evening. No air was getting into Parchment House. The place was like a sealed box.

He stood in the shadowy chaos of the dining room. A crack of light shone between the shutters. As far as the Reverend was concerned there was no one out there anymore. Orphans, Worthies, the robot: All were things from another world. The only people left in this particular world were himself and Johnnie Rattle.

Reverend Slipper picked up the discarded carving knife from the dining room floor, and, with the point, started to clean every scrap of dirt from beneath his slightly long and sharp fingernails. When he had finished he put the carving knife in his pocket. All the time he was humming and humming, silently, down inside himself. It was as if he had a thermostat inside him that had broken down and all he could do now was to get hotter and hotter until he boiled over.

He noticed that his eyes were beginning to pierce the gloom, his ears were picking up sounds they had never heard before—deathwatch beetles clacking in the woodwork, ancient soot shifting behind the blocked-up fireplace. The whole house was bolted up. Nobody could get in and nobody could get out. Upstairs was Johnnie Rattle, all tied up. There could be no mercy for him now. None whatsoever.

Inside his head Reverend Slipper heard a singing start up, as of a celestial choir.

18
HIDE-AND-SEEK

Johnnie's head felt like an enormous black turnip. The handkerchief around his eyes smelled of dead mice. For a long time he lay under the bed where he had been shoved, unable to move, unable to think at all. Then, unseen by him, a small green spider crawled over the leaves of the geranium, swung down to the floor, and then started to scuttle toward Johnnie. It clambered up his shoulder and then began to run over his face as he lay there in the dark. The sensation of the tiny feet running over his cheek seemed to wake him from his stupor.

"I'm not going to lie here like a sacrifice, just waiting for Reverend Slipper to turn up," he said to himself, and rolled out from under the bed. "Maybe if I can manage to get downstairs I can show the Governors what Reverend Slipper has done to me."

The only way he could move was by pushing his tied-up feet forward and then pulling the rest of his body after them. He decided to use the cracks between the floorboards, which he could just feel through his thin canvas shoes, to keep a straight line toward the door. It was hard work, but eventually he made it. Just outside the door were the stairs. Inside his head he could see the steep drop, falling away like the side of a mountain. He stuck his feet over the edge and started to bump and shuffle down, but at the bend he slipped and was tossed headlong, banging himself all over and landing with a crash at the bottom.

He lay there with all the breath knocked out of his body. At any moment he expected to hear the Reverend's footsteps approaching. Far away, muffled through the handkerchief, he heard a banging and a rattling that seemed to come from outside. Then there was silence.

Where was everybody? Where were the Governors? Where was Reverend Slipper?

Whatever had happened, it was no good lying in the middle of the corridor like an undelivered parcel. He would have to move. But where? Was there nowhere to hide? Was there no way of loosening the ropes?

Suddenly an image came into Johnnie's head. It hung there in the darkness: a long black leather box, with the inscription, "To B. Slipper from his Dear Mother on the Occasion of his Diploma in Moral

Studies." That leather box lay next to the Worship Transistor on a shelf in the Reverend's room, just down the corridor. Inside the box was the cut-throat razor which every morning left the Reverend's throat and chin as smooth as a slab of marble.

"If I can get hold of that razor," said Johnnie to himself, "I might just possibly be able to escape."

He rolled toward the Reverend's room. Luckily the door was ajar. He could tell it was the right place because of the smell. He paused on the threshold, listening. It was like putting one's head into a crocodile's mouth, entering the Reverend's room. There was silence. Taking a deep breath, Johnnie rolled through the doorway and then started to make for the shelf where the cut-throat razor was kept. A couple of times he lost his bearings and bumped into things, but at last his feet got entangled in the wires that hung from the Worship Transistor. The shelf with the black box was just overhead.

It was immensely difficult, all tied up as he was, to maneuver himself upright, but he managed at last. He felt along the shelf with his chin. *Where was it?* Ah yes, there was the edge.

As Johnnie pushed the box on to the floor with his chin a voice started intoning just above his head:

"Ne'er mind how far is the farthest star
No matter how weary and sad we are
Humble civilians we stumble on
In the valiant army though hope be gone . . ."

For a terrible moment Johnnie thought it was Reverend Slipper! But then he realized he must have accidentally nudged the button that set off the Worship Transistor. Oh, please, please, make that awful racket stop! Desperately he searched with his chin . . .

127

"In the Land of Ganda we prostrate kneel
And wondrous happiness all do feel
The sun it shineth the moon gives light
And giveth contentedness day and night . . ."

"Oh, shut up, shut up, shut up," whispered Johnnie through gritted teeth, searching wildly for the button with his chin. Ah, there it was at last. . . . He gave it a desperate thump.

"The once guilty natives are . . ."

PING.

Thank goodness.

Johnnie slithered to the ground and felt around until he found the case, unhooked it with his nose and took out the razor with his teeth. He managed to grip the handle tight and sawed at the ropes binding his chest. It was difficult to use any force at this angle, but the blade of the razor was so sharp it went through the fiber like a scalpel cutting silk.

The rope was fraying and loosening. The muscles of Johnnie's jaw ached and ached with gripping the handle of the razor, but just as he was about to drop the thing, the rope around his chest and shoulders suddenly gave way. It unwound in a great coil, and immediately the bonds around his wrists loosened, so that he was able to pull free his hands. He tore off the blindfold. He was just bending over to untie his ankles when he heard steps coming up the stairs.

He would know those steps anywhere.

The steps stopped outside in the corridor. Johnnie could see a shadow darkening the wall outside the half-open door. Then the shadow moved. The footsteps went on up the attic stairs. At last Johnnie managed to pull the ropes off his ankles. He shook them free, then picked up ropes, razor, box, and handkerchief and shoved them far out of sight behind the divan. To his horror he heard the steps coming down the attic stairs, great bounds of steps. He should have run downstairs immediately. He shouldn't have tried to cover his traces. By now he could have been outside, running across the lawn. But it was too late to think of that. He crouched behind the door and listened.

Reverend Slipper was really on the warpath now. Johnnie heard the man go into the schoolroom. A door opened and something heavy fell to the floor—an iron chair. He must be looking in the cupboard. Johnnie ran out of Reverend Slipper's room and headed for the stairs, but he heard the Reverend coming across the schoolroom, so he darted through the nearest door, to get out of sight, quick quick. . . .

He found himself in big Marvin's room—the door was unlocked! The place was almost completely bare— big Marvin must be a hermit! No furniture, no possessions, nothing but a big bare bed with its striped mattress in the middle of the room, and rows of empty shelves. There was nowhere to hide in here.

Reverend Slipper's footsteps went past big Marvin's room. The man must be going to the laundry. One, two, three, yes, he must be nearly there, he would be rummaging through the great linen cupboard, now was the only chance . . .

Johnnie ran out of big Marvin's room and down the stairs as quietly and as fast as he could. Perhaps now he could slip out through an unlocked door and be away, down the road . . . but he ran smack into darkness. For a moment it was like being blindfolded again. Then he made out the gleam of the long steel bars across the front door and the trembling streak of blue between the shutters. There was no sound, except for a tap dripping and dripping.

He crept along the corridor to the back of the house. Through the open door of the dining room he could just make out the blue mounds of the ruined feast. Insects were swarming all over it, humming like miniature generators. Through the crack between the shutters he could see again the chink of blue, lighter than inside, but darkening every second.

Footsteps were coming down the stairs.

He ran into the kitchen and pulled at the door. He scrambled at the lock, then searched wildly for the key. He tried to cry out, for he could hear a faint rustling from outside: "Solly ... Philly ... Anna ... help, help ..."

He wanted to shout, but fear had made his voice come out in a croaky whisper. He tried to hammer on the door, but it was as if his fists were made out of water. Reverend Slipper was close. Johnnie could feel it. He could feel that presence everywhere. "Oh, please, oh, please ..." he whispered, scrabbling at the door.

The only hope was to try and activate the mechanism that worked the shutters and to plunge out through the window. He ran over to the Control Panel and started, in the dark, to push at every button, trying to find the secret combination. Maybe something would open the shutters, unlock the door, bang the gong, summon help, blow up the house, anything ...

But his crazed pushing of buttons started off all the gadgets at once. Lights flashed on and off. Doughnuts and hamburgers began to shoot out of the top of the Protibar, and soup leaked and poured unstoppably from the trap at the bottom. The Flydevora whizzed around and around frantically and then began to unwind all over the room in slow silver tendrils that sparked and curled around the kitchen, at the same time flinging a cloud of insect corpses into the air. A mush of bubbles oozed from the Omnikleen and the Kleenukwik, and spread out around the legs of the kitchen table. Johnnie pushed buttons frantically, trying now to get the mechanisms to stop, but it just got worse. All over the house he could hear machines starting up, whirring and gurgling and making noises like zips and springs breaking. Things started to smoke, then the lights all blazed up and then with a great *prang* everything blew completely, and Johnnie was left standing in the darkness in the smoking, swampy kitchen. Amid the noise of dozens of machines gradually running out of steam, he heard footsteps coming along the corridor. There was nowhere to hide but the pantry. He pulled the big rusty bolt and tore open the door and threw himself into the feathery dungeon and buried himself behind a pile of sacks. He heard Reverend Slipper come into the kitchen. The man just stood there.

"The Wreck of the Hesperus. The Walls of Jericho. What a disgraceful mess. What I would have expected. The worm in the apple has been at work here. The whole crop is in danger of infection. Now, where's the right drawer? Ah yes, here we are, I have it . . . and it . . . and them. . . ."

Crouched in the pantry, scarcely daring to breathe, Johnnie heard the scrape of a match, then a faint light came through the torn grille and glimmered on the pantry wall.

"I know exactly what's what. Ha, ha, ha," muttered Reverend Slipper. He hissed a little, stalking around the kitchen, and tut-tutting about the state of the floor.

Johnnie crouched even lower behind the Feather Bags. Perhaps Reverend Slipper would think he had escaped, perhaps he might go searching out the front of the house and leave the door open, perhaps . . .

A feather drifted up Johnnie's nose. He could feel

it tickling his nostrils. He brushed it away. Tears came into his eyes, he fought against the sneeze he could feel starting to explode, good, it was subsiding, it had gone, thank goodness . . .

The pantry door creaked open. A dim light flickered over the filthy walls. The light went up and down, back up, then down, it was shining directly at Johnnie Rattle, he shrank back into the soft sacks, he closed his eyes . . .

Reverend Slipper sprang.

Johnnie Rattle fought like a wild cat. He scratched and bit and butted with his head. Feathers flew in all directions. The whole pantry was adrift with them. But Reverend Slipper had him in a grip that could never be escaped.

Johnnie Rattle was caught at last.

19
A CANDLE AND A KNIFE

Reverend Slipper held the candle in one hand, while the other was clamped on the back of Johnnie's neck. The candle was in a pewter holder in the form of a pixie, with an upturned acorn on its head. As they climbed the stairs the candlelight made their shadows streak and flicker on the wall. Reverend Slipper marched Johnnie along the corridor and into the schoolroom.

The man locked the door behind him and put the key in his pocket. He sat at the table on the platform. He made Johnnie sit at the desk opposite, in the front row. In the flickering light, Johnnie could make out the scratched names of generations of orphans. They left no messages, no jokes, only their names.

Reverend Slipper took the carving knife out of his pocket and once more scraped the point under his by now immaculate nails. He had set the candle on the windowsill, so that he was in shadow. The candle made a soft hissing sound as it burned down. Long streamers of wax floated slowly down its sides and all over the pewter pixie.

"You couldn't get out, could you?" said Reverend Slipper at last. "You tried all the doors and shutters, but you couldn't get out. You couldn't get out now, not at all, even if you were free to try, which you are not, of course. I knew you couldn't get out, could never get out. That was why I was in no hurry."

"In no hurry for what?"

"For anything. I've got all the time in the world."

It was warm in the schoolroom. Johnnie's head felt heavy. From far away, as if from another world, he heard the rumble of thunder. There was a faint rustle of leaves. But the night grew hotter still. The sound of thunder came from farther away; the sound of the leaves stopped. It was as if he and Reverend Slipper were cocooned in a spaceship, far out in the galaxy.

"You see," said Reverend Slipper, "everything is your fault."

"*Mine?*"

"Look here," said Reverend Slipper, "you can take that look of injured innocence off your face to start with. It won't wash with me. Somebody is always to blame. I found no difficulty, when casting around in my mind, in recognizing that you are the one—you are the snake in Paradise, which must be cast out. It's as simple as that. It is for that reason that you are here tonight."

"What do you mean?"

"You are here because you have been sent to me so that I can punish you and thus rid Parchment House of the scourge of your presence. Before you we had generation upon generation of happy orphans all sailing off to Ganda Ganda and Balyhoo Bala with never a word of complaint—with, if the truth be told, in many cases a happy song upon their lips. And yet—when did you arrive?"

"I don't know."

"Where were you before?"

"I don't remember."

"There you are, then," said Reverend Slipper triumphantly. "Complete amnesia, the sure sign of a guilty conscience. Well, whatever cesspool you sprang from, since you arrived at Parchment House things have gone from bad to worse. This downward spiral must end!"

"What are you . . . ?"

"You have the right," said Reverend Slipper, "to remain silent. I strongly advise you to exercise that right."

The Reverend was beginning to feel better. The red band around his head had loosened and the blood in his veins coursed sweetly. Once he had dealt with this matter he could invite the Governors to come up and see the reformed Parchment House, with discipline twice as efficient as before, with all laxity eliminated. . . .

"It is primarily *what you are!*" shouted the Reverend suddenly, beating the air with the carving knife. "You are not grateful and humble, you are wicked and proud. What you do is known as biting the hand that feeds you. Your very existence lowers the tone of the establishment. And it is not only Parchment House that is threatened. Just imagine if the whole world was filled with people like yourself. What would happen to all us upright citizens? You would destroy us! I can see it in your eyes! The whole system would disintegrate! Why should you think that you, a minor cog in a vast, smooth-running machine, should be allowed to sabotage the whole mechanism? Why, your little friend Solly Turk had the temerity to ask for chocolates this afternoon. Chocolates! For orphans! After the fiasco of the day! I never heard anything like it!"

"What's wrong with wanting chocolates?" asked Johnnie, feeling it was safer to keep the Reverend talking.

"That's just it. You just can't *see* what's wrong. You have not understood the first thing of what we have tried to teach you here. It is a pity that you will have no chance to mature and thus just possibly find out the error of your ways. However, shut your mouth. I'm tired of the sound that comes out of it. If you open it again, I shall cut off your lips with this special self-sharpening knife."

The Reverend stared at Johnnie as if he was looking straight through him into the shadows at the back of the schoolroom. The candle was guttering lower and lower.

"Aha!" said Reverend Slipper. "Silence at last. I hope this betrays a morsel of repentance. It is better to repent than not, even at the last minute. Though it makes no difference to the outcome. Now, I'm going to tell you what I'm going to do. I'm going to get rid of you, fairly quickly and painlessly, as it is not morally correct to linger over these things. Then I shall put your disposable remains into the cupboard behind me, under all the piles and piles of notebooks that so impressed our visitors. Then I shall lock the cupboard door forever. After this, Parchment House will once more be open to the public, ready to embrace future generations of orphans. The place will be cleansed both morally and physically. I shall order seventy cartons of dust cloths and we shall clean the place from top to toe, and I shall renew my subscription to that wonderful periodical, *Good News from the Orphan Front*. I shall tell you how long we have to say good-bye—until the candle burns to its end. Look on the candle as a metaphor for your brief and miserable life. Everything is sad, but for the best. Ah, well!"

Reverend Slipper looked in the breast pocket of his jacket for the black handkerchief and then remembered that he had used it to blindfold Johnnie. He buffed the blade of the knife on his sleeve instead, until the metal shone.

Johnnie had spotted that the schoolroom window was fractionally open. He managed to leap across the room and throw wide the window before Reverend Slipper had realized what had happened. He hauled himself up on to the ledge. For a moment he hesitated, right on the edge of the sill, appalled at the great bowl of darkness beneath. This second of hesitation allowed the Reverend to dart across and grab him. Johnnie tried to launch himself over the edge. For a moment he hung in midair, legs thrashing, held only by the man's relentlessly powerful grip.

"Help me!" cried Johnnie. "Help! Quickly, quickly! *Help!*"

It seemed to him as if his words were blown away into the night, to vanish forever.

Reverend Slipper pulled him back into the room.

"Now don't do anything stupid. Resign yourself to fate. That has always been one of your troubles; you will *not* resign yourself to fate. Still, console yourself that your troubles will soon be over forever."

He made Johnnie stand beside the platform and held the knife against the small of his back. They watched the candle growing smaller and more lopsided, hissing quietly to itself. The window was still open. Like a black curtain, undecorated with stars or moon, the night hung behind the candle. Then another light darted through the air, illuminating the fruit trees and the spiked point of the pagoda roof. The lightning danced around the house. In spite of his terror, Johnnie found himself counting inwardly to find out how far away the thunder was. Seven miles.

Reverend Slipper gave a small sigh.

"I suppose that is why my head is so bad. Thunder in the air always has that effect on me. After all this is over I must get Mrs. Padlock to mix me up some of her headache powders."

Again the lightning darted through the garden. For a moment the distant horizon was a queer pinky color. The candle flame streaked sideways, sank right down and seemed about to go out; but after a second it rallied and lifted itself straight again, though it was nearly burned down to its end.

"Not too long to wait now," said Reverend Slipper. "And then we can get back to normal."

20
A FLASH OF LIGHTNING

All afternoon the orphans sat in the vegetable garden, watching the back of Parchment House. The black shutters over the downstairs windows looked like eyepatches, and the upper windows looked like blind eyes, the glass scarcely reflecting anything.

In the pagoda Percival Amalgam fidgeted and whined, but eventually fell asleep on the floor, while Mrs. Padlock kept guard beside him, her brain seething with thoughts of the revenge to be wreaked on the orphans once Reverend Slipper opened up the house. But the house stayed shut.

As dusk came down, swarms of gnats invaded the garden and hung about the children's heads. They brushed them away, and still did not move. After the gnats, when it grew darker still, moths went bobbing over the vegetable beds, and other hidden insects buzzed and hummed and crawled over the ground and zigzagged in the air. A fox ran through the little meadow behind the pagoda, but so quickly and quietly that no one saw it. No cars passed along the road in front of the house. Scarcely any lights shone on the horizon.

It grew hotter. The children took off their rummage sale shirts and sweaters, but still they sweated. The thin Twins fell asleep, their cheeks against the warm earth, and Alice whimpered that she was frightened and wanted to go back to the attic. But the rest of the children just kept quiet, their mouths open, their eyes staring straight ahead. Tiggy sat behind a bush, growling to herself. Only Inky Dumb-Dumb, who all day had been huddling against trees or in corners whenever he could, seemed to have lost interest in everything. He lay in the nettle bed, not heeding the stings, his arms over his head. Solly sat beside the robot in the beet patch. Archibald's metallic body gleamed in the dusk, though it was difficult to know where the reflections came from. Solly put his hand on the robot's foot. It felt cold and dead, like a broken gadget.

The night grew hotter still.

Suddenly there was a tremendous commotion in the house, and the lights started to flash on and off. Then with a colossal rumble everything went dark again. The children peered at the great hulk of Parchment House. A wavering light appeared in the schoolroom window. Tiggy stood up, her chin jutting forward. She pointed at the window. "Look! Look! It's a . . . a . . ." The children stared upward intently, but nothing happened. In silence they watched the wavering light. The faint burr of a voice came from inside the house.

What was happening?

Behind them, all around them, the children heard the thunder rolling. Though it was soft and far away, they felt the ground tremble. Then suddenly, without any warning, the window was flung open and a small form appeared silhouetted on the sill, but as it hesitated, about to jump, a far larger silhouette appeared behind.

The large form seized the small form, held it out over the darkness, then pulled it back in.

They heard the cry: "Help! Quickly, quickly! *Help!*"

Solly ran up to the house. He shook and banged on the door, but it would not budge. He tore at the shutters over the dining room window, tugged them, beat them and shook them, but the things were fastened immovably. He hung on to one of the shutters and pulled with all his weight, but it made no difference at all. The shutters were made of iron and would not shift an inch.

All the children ran up and started beating on the side of the house, while their eyes stared up toward the light still flickering in the window. A great wail came from them.

"What shall we do? Oh, what shall we do?"

Only Inky Dumb-Dumb did not move, but still lay like a heap of rags in the nettle bed.

Solly looked around in desperation, as if he wanted to summon a magician out of the air. His eye was caught by the slightly glowing form in the beet bed.

"Archibald!" shouted Solly. "We must use Archibald!"

All the children collected around the capsized robot. They pulled it to its feet. It tottered, but they held it

141

upright. The thing felt like a tower of old tin cans. It swayed and clattered. "Come on!" they whispered. "Wake up, Archibald!" They rubbed its metal. They rocked its limbs as if that would encourage it to spring to life. Solly shouted into the microphone and jabbed his finger over and over on the START button, but the thing seemed to have no power at all. They shook it and shook it. But the battery seemed completely dead.

Grub had his arms around one leg and Jackie was holding the other and they were jumping up and down, but all they were doing was making Archibald clank and totter even more.

Then Jane Pegg said, "Inky Dumb-Dumb should help. I'll go and get him."

She trotted over to Inky and picked him up, brought him back, and set him in front of the robot.

"You've got to help too, Inky. Even if you can't talk, I know you understand. Reverend Slipper is going to hurt Johnnie Rattle, and Archibald has got to help us save him. So you've got to help Archibald."

"Oh, it's no good asking *him*," said Solly Turk. "He can't help nobody, not even himself."

Inky Dumb-Dumb stood staring at Archibald.

Suddenly an extraordinary, rusty, strangulated cry filled the vegetable garden.

"HA . . . HA . . . HA . . ."

"Inky Dumb-Dumb's trying to say something!" said Jane Pegg.

"HA . . . HA . . . HA . . ."

"You shouldn't *laugh*, Inky," said Anna Daw in a horrified whisper.

The children stared at him. His voice seemed to be coming out of a hole in the ground. They could hardly see him, but they could just make out his fists beating his sides, and the black *O* of his mouth gaping.

142

"HA . . . HA . . . HARCHIBALL!" yelled Inky at the top of his voice, and fell in a heap on the ground.

Something happened to the robot. It gave a jerk and then a twitter. Solly put his head to the robot's chest. There was a faint, faint humming—so faint that he couldn't be sure it wasn't the sound of the night insects all around.

"*Start*, Archibald!" he whispered over and over.

He looked up into the robot's eye. There seemed to be a tiny red light in the middle of the metal ball.

Philadelphia suddenly shouted, "Come on, we must use all our forces, we must think very hard about one thing, everybody must think about Johnnie Rattle. Ready, set, *go!*"

The orphans packed so close around Archibald that the smallest ones, right down near the knees, were in danger of being squashed. Everyone thought of only one thing: Johnnie Rattle. Johnnie Rattle, Johnnie Rattle!

It was as if all the power of the district was suddenly concentrated on this one spot. The humming inside the robot got louder. The metal of its body grew warmer. It shivered all over and then gave a great jerk that shook most of the children off into the beet bed.

"Let him go!" cried Solly Turk.

The robot was standing with its own power now.

A crack of lightning ran around the garden.

"Archibald," said Solly into the microphone, "you're not working for them Worthies no more, it's *us* what you've got to help. You've got to go in there and rescue Johnnie Rattle. You go get Johnnie Rattle! You save him, Archibald! You're the only one can do it!"

He pressed the START button. Archibald lurched forward.

From the pagoda they heard Mrs. Padlock cry,

"Stop that robot immediately! It's got to be dismantled! Stop it, I say, stop the robot at once!"

She was too late.

Another whipcrack of lightning ran around the garden. In its eerie glow Archibald looked like a giant.

Shining in the dark, Archibald strode up to the house. He went straight to the dining room window and, lifting a mighty arm, tore off one of the shutters and then the other as easily as if he was tearing sheets off a notepad. Then the two big-fisted hands shook the whole window frame out of its socket, as easily as if it had been a thin piece of ice over a puddle. Archibald laid the frame and unbroken glass neatly beside the rain barrel and then, without hesitation, climbed through the black hole left in the side of the house.

The children stayed in the garden, looking toward the candle flickering in the open window. The flame was guttering; there was scarcely any candle left. They started chanting softly, and then a little louder: "Archibald! Archibald! Archibald!"

There was a splintering noise from up above, and a cry of rage. Then a terrible scream rang out.

"I shall have you turned into bootscrapers for this!"

A dark form appeared in the window, a silhouette that was not distinguishable as man or beast. A knife was brandished, a plume waved, a giant hand grabbed for a bony head. Some terrible struggle was going on. The candle tipped over and went out.

Then a body was thrown out of the window. The body corkscrewed through the air before landing on the Bird Table with a great *splat* that was like the sound of a wet towel being slapped against a wall. For a moment it lay on the Bird Table, its legs dangling over the edge.

Then suddenly the whole garden was filled with an enormous Shape that later some said was feathered, some said was bony, and still others said was like smoke from a bonfire, but which all agreed made no noise.

A great jag of lightning lit up the garden, and in its glow the Shape could be seen to have vast dragonish wings and a long head, with a beak shaped like pruning shears which was at that moment in the process of lifting the limp body off the Bird Table and making off with it, for reasons best known to itself.

(Nobody was sure which direction the Shape flew off in: Some thought it flew low over the pagoda, and then inland; others were sure it had lifted its burden over the roof of Parchment House and flown away toward the sea.)

The flash of lightning that had lit up the Shape at the same moment fastened on a great plumed figure still standing in the schoolroom window and lit it up in a sheet of flame. Then with one big bang the lightning vanished, as did the giant figure itself, falling back into the schoolroom, leaving the window blank.

The thunderclap came almost immediately afterward. Leaves began to rustle, and from far off, then close, came the sound of rain, and soon the rain itself, sweeping right through the garden.

In a great crowd the children ran through the hole in the wall and up to the first floor. They stepped through the splintered door. There on the floor in the dark they found Johnnie Rattle, stunned but not harmed. All that remained of Archibald was a heavy chunk of mangled black compacted metal which had once been his body. His head, which had miraculously escaped the lightning undamaged, had rolled away to the back of the schoolroom.

21
THE TOWER

Three days later the children carried the Feather Bags and what remained of Archibald's body to the little meadow behind the pagoda. Right in the center of the meadow they cut out a patch of grass and orchids, and dug a hole. They laid the black chunk of metal in the hole and covered it with feathers. Then they put back the patch of turf. Except for a small seam in the earth, no one could know that the ground had been disturbed.

When they got back to Parchment House they

opened all the doors and windows, and sat watching the last swallows collecting on the wires.

By the time the first autumn frost had arrived in Carstairs and Bungho, Parchment House was in chaos. All the gadgets had been torn to bits and the pieces turned into tunnels and dens. The fridge had long since been broken into and the chocolates eaten. The younger children had grown sick eating doughnuts and drinking kiwi juice. Now they lived off the half-processed supplies left at the house by the delivery trucks, which still called weekly, no one having told them to stop. There were heaps of food lying everywhere, molding and smelling bad.

The children held a meeting. They decided to write to the Authorities, telling them of all they had endured, and pleading that such things should never happen again. A new kind of orphanage should be created, where children should have freedom, good food, and no Moral Homilies whatsoever—and no rummage sale clothes. No more boatloads of orphans should be sent off to distant outposts, and all communications with Balyhoo Bala, Hideyhangoo, and the Ganda Ganda Territories should cease forthwith, except for Christmas cards.

The sudden disappearance of an entire batch of Worthies (for Mrs. Padlock had not been seen since the night of the carrying off of Reverend Slipper), quite apart from the orphans' complaints, was such an odd occurrence that the Authorities feared a major scandal. They argued among themselves, but could come to no decision at all. The local Orphan Policy was in ruins.

Then something wonderful and surprising happened.

One day, not long after the letter to the Authorities

had been sent, the rag-and-bone man stopped his cart by the gate, and unloaded a passenger who had been traveling balanced on top of an old fridge. The passenger walked slowly up the path, carrying a small heap of possessions in a handkerchief. He looked all about him as if he was searching for something. The children were playing on the lawn. Solly Turk went white, then red, and ran up to the man shouting, *"It's my dad!"*

Solly's dad, once he had had some cake and a good sleep, proved to be just the right person for Parchment House. He was good at football and cricket, and knew all about carpentry, dinosaurs, and stars, not to mention being a qualified acrobat and a brilliant cook.

The orphans immediately composed a second letter to the Authorities, saying that Solly Turk's dad was the only suitable person to look after orphans. If he was not appointed they would all descend on Carstairs and Bungho and create havoc. The letter was signed by all the children, even Inky Dumb-Dumb, who signed with a blot.

The Authorities agreed at once. It seemed the obvious solution. They hoped they would not have to think anymore about Parchment House for many a long day.

And as for Mrs. Padlock and Percival? Well, Mrs. Padlock had only a vague notion of what had happened on the night of the thunderstorm, but whatever it was, she knew life would never be the same again. Seizing Percival's plump hand she pulled him through the hedge and made for the main road by a roundabout route. Once there they had hitched a ride with first of all a milk van, then a truck carrying coal, and finally a long-distance transporter of frozen cheeseburgers. They traveled all the way to Blackpool, where Mrs. Padlock got a job as a waitress, serving tea to old ladies while a small string orchestra played old-time music on a stage decorated with potted palms and swiss cheese plants. Mrs. Padlock wore a black dress and a frilly apron and hat, and she took everyone back to the old days, so that she got a lot of tips and was able to support Percival Amalgam, who is still as fat and useless as ever. He lies on his bed in the boardinghouse where he lives with Mrs. Padlock, eating ice cream and telling the landlady, when she comes in to do his room, that Mrs. Padlock has stolen him away from his mom and dad, who are Hollywood movie stars, because she is hoping for a ransom. And the landlady shakes out her duster so that the fluff goes all over Percival's ice cream. She feels sorry for Mrs. Padlock. As well she might.

On one of the fine autumn days, early in the morning, Johnnie Rattle took the head of Archibald from where it had been kept on the bed in big Marvin's room. He wrapped it in silver foil and tied around it a net of string. He set out before most of the orphans were up, though Jackie and Grub were already raiding the cake supplies, and Solly Turk was sitting at the top of a magnolia tree playing a tune on a hand-carved whistle.

Instead of taking the road to Carstairs and Bungho, Johnnie crossed the fields that lay beyond the side of the house. He was going to the small forest that he had looked at for so long from his window.

It took a long time to cross the fields, jumping over small streams, crawling over walls and under wire, and inching his way around a patch of marsh; but at last he found himself on the edge of the forest. He could see the top of the tower right in the middle of the trees, but once he had entered the gloom beneath the branches it kept vanishing and then appearing again where he had not been expecting it. Finally it disappeared altogether, and Johnnie was just beginning to think he had lost his way when, coming along a path which suddenly bent between two enormous trees, he found himself in a clearing, in the middle of which was the tower.

Its stones still sparkled with frost. Only a few rays of sun penetrated through the tree branches, though light glinted on the golden weathercock at the top of the pointed roof. A weather-beaten turquoise door was set in an arch at the base of the tower. The only window, small and round, was right at the top, just underneath the roof; but all the way up the wall, set seemingly at random in the stone, were small niches in which stood carvings—a lion, a dove, a unicorn and, highest of all, a mermaid holding a crown.

Johnnie pushed open the door and climbed the winding staircase. It was so dark he had to steady himself against the wall, so that when he got to the top his fingertips were covered with green powder. At the top of the tower was a small round room, with stone walls and a wooden floor covered with scuffed dust. A ray of sunlight shone through the window, leaving a circle of brightness on the floor. Johnnie laid Archibald's head in the patch of sun, then looked about him.

Someone had been living in this room—or had just moved in. Heaps of cloth were piled against the wall, and there were three vast chests, their big locks formed in the shape of flames. Johnnie went over to the chests. He ran his hand over the old wood, then carefully tried one of the lids. It lifted with a faint rasp. Inside, the wood was lined with mirror glass, so that the contents were reflected to and fro, and it was difficult to know what was real and what was reflection. Even the bottom of the chest was lined with glass, so it was like looking into a well. The objects that were packed inside, delicately balanced one against the other, were like nothing that Johnnie had ever seen—small carvings, glass tubes and siphons, lumps of red dirt, twigs spangly with crystals. . . . A faint crackling was coming from the chest, as if it was full of tiny living things, insects perhaps, that were shifting under his gaze. Johnnie closed the lid. He felt he had been looking at something secret and strange.

There was little else in the room. On a hook on the wall hung a big black hat, and on the floor beneath was a kingfisher in a glass case. That was all there was.

Yes, thought Johnnie, this is the right place for Archibald's head.

He looked out through the tower window. There, far away, was the side of Parchment House, with the window of his cubicle only a speck at this distance. The window in the tower was like the twin of his. In that faraway window the red geranium was growing in the sun.

He unwrapped Archibald's head and, holding it level with his own head, looked into the robot's eye. The metal was slightly warm. Sun came through the glass and glinted on the eyeball. Johnnie stared at what remained of Archibald. As he stared, it seemed that the metal was becoming liquid, like mercury. He peered harder and could just see, deep in the center of the eyeball, no bigger than a baby's fingernail, a swirling cone of flames.

Archibald's head hissed slightly, then the lid with its stiff fringe of lashes clacked down over the eyeball. When it lifted, the eyeball was blank again. Johnnie could feel a tremor pass up his arms. He put down the head for a moment while he pulled over the kingfisher in its glass case and set it beneath the window. It was just the right height. He put the robot's head on the case.

The robot and the kingfisher seemed to be good

companions for each other, the kingfisher staring back into the room, the head looking out over the top of the forest toward the round window of Parchment House.

"Good-bye, Archibald."

Johnnie walked slowly home. A slight wind was blowing the oat grass in the fields. A kestrel, balancing itself with its long tail, trembled against the sky. As he came near to Parchment House he could hear the sound of children playing cricket on the lawn.